ROTHKO'S RED

SUE HUBBARD is a freelance art critic, novelist and poet. Twice winner of the London Writers competition she was the Poetry Society's first Public Art Poet. Her first collection *Everything Begins with the Skin* was published in 1994 by Enitharmon. A number of her poems appeared in Oxford Poets 2000 published by Carcanet. *Depth of Field*, her first novel, was published by Dewi Lewis in 2000. John Berger called it a 'remarkable first novel.' She writes a regular column in *The Independent*.

Also by Sue Hubbard

Everything Begins with the Skin (Enitharmon, 1994;
   Salt 2009)
Depth of Field (Dewy Lewis, 2000)
Ghost Station (Salt, 2004)

SUE HUBBARD
ROTHKO'S RED

CAMBRIDGE

PUBLISHED BY SALT PUBLISHING
14a High Street, Fulbourn, Cambridge CB21 5DH United Kingdom

© Sue Hubbard, 2008

The right of Sue Hubbard to be identified as the
author of this work has been asserted by her in accordance
with Section 77 of the Copyright, Designs and Patents Act 1988.

First published 2008

Printed and bound in the United Kingdom by Biddles Ltd, King's Lynn, Norfolk

Typeset in Swift 10 / 14

ISBN 978 1 84471 444 5 hardback

Salt Publishing Ltd gratefully acknowledges
the financial assistance of Arts Council England

1 3 5 7 9 8 6 4 2

For Louie and Alena

Contents

Rothko's Red	1
Mona Lisa	20
Jackson Pollock's Curtains	30
The Monarch of the Glen	42
Mondrian's Moon	56
Bernini and Leopard Skin	77
Goya's Dark	94
Oi Yoi Yoi	111
The Hay Wain	122
The Laughing Cavalier	137

ROTHKO'S RED

'It's like your cunt,' he'd whispered in her ear in front of the magenta Rothko. 'All that velvety redness. I know it so well; every fold and crevice. I don't have to be an expert on art to understand these paintings.'

He had been standing behind her in front of the large canvas, his arms wrapped around her waist, his newly shaved chin on her shoulder, as she'd talked him through Abstract Expressionism. She'd liked standing like that in a public space, the bulk of him pressed against her back, their smells mingling. She had felt, what? Owned. Later when they'd gone back to the little hotel room with the low ceiling in the Marais and made love in the afternoon, the shrieks of the children in the playground of the cole Maternelle below had floated up through their window. He had brought her to Paris for her birthday and they'd sat in a small side street outside a café in the April sunlight drinking *café au lait*.

'When I was trapped in my marriage, this is what I dreamt of,' he'd said. 'Sitting having breakfast in Paris with a beautiful woman.' No one had said anything like that to her before, none of the occasional lovers who had crossed her path when she'd been living alone, trying to make ends meet, struggling to bring up Suzie. They had only been together for two months. On the journey back to London on the Eurostar she'd watched their joint reflection in the train's dark glass whilst he'd slept, her head resting on his shoulder, trying to seal the image in her mind like those fossilised flies in amber that the Algerian trader had wanted to sell them on the steps of the Musée D'Orsay; though the amber, laid in rows on a rush mat, had probably been plastic, the flies fake. But they had looked good together. Not quite young anymore, it was true, but an attractive item. And as he'd slept, she'd been conscious of the need to file and catalogue the moment, aware of its transformation from the present into a memory.

～

Belle was waiting for Maggie under the clock at Grand Central station. The concourse was busy. It was snowing outside and Manhattan had become gridlocked. Commuters scurried to catch their out of town trains before the weather got worse, hurrying to their platforms beneath the crystal chandeliers across the marble halls as the large flakes of snow slowly melted on their hats and scarves. Belle was reading a book, her coat collar pulled up against the icy February chill. The tweed cloth was covered in cats' hairs and there was a small hole in the toe of her shoe. She looked up from her reading as Maggie approached and broke into a smile.

'Hi, you must be Maggie, great to meet you.'

Maggie lent forward, relieved, and kissed her on the cheek. Belle was Adam's cousin once removed on his American mother's side. When Adam had been twelve his father had sent him to stay with Belle's family up in their cabin in the Adirondacks. Adam had often wondered if it was supposed to have been some sort of consolation prize that holiday, compensation for his mother's sudden death on that rainy night in that terrible pile up on the M4. His father had never really been able to talk about it, had retreated into the carapace of his own grief, leaving the boys to cope the best they could. He was also a believer in the redeeming power of physical activity. He had thought it was good for both young bodies and minds, especially as Adam and his younger brother, Tom, lived in Fulham. So that summer they had been packed off for a month in the States. They had fished and canoed, had made campfires down by the lake, and Adam had tried not to think about his dead mother.

During the funeral service at the crematorium, a vicar whom Adam had never met before had compared his mother's earthly life to the state of an unborn baby, explaining that a baby lived in a safe environment, blissfully unaware of what fate awaited it once it was pushed out from its warm watery cradle into the wide world. The baby, the vicar had said, was without fear for its future.

And while, in life, we might think we had an idea of what death might entail, we could not possibly conceive of the journey into the light that would follow, imagine the comfort that would engulf us, any more than the baby could imagine being born. For as with infinity, the human mind could not comprehend the mysteries that belonged only to God.

Adam had tried to listen, but had felt nothing. He was sure they were supposed to be comforting, but the vicar's words hadn't helped very much. He had bit his lip hard, hoping the pain would stop him crying. He just wanted his mother back.

That summer in the Adirondacks Adam had thought Belle a bit odd. There had been something intense about her, something of the outsider. Although only thirteen, she was already taller than him, with long shin bones and gangly arms and small new breasts that grazed the blue nylon of her baggy shapeless swimsuit. She'd been physically inept, always losing her sneakers or stepping on glass or dropping her swimming costume out of the roll of her towel as they'd gone down to bathe off the wooden jetty in the cold lake. But she had been funny. He'd liked that about her, though perhaps it had been a bid for acceptance, an apology for her clumsiness, but she'd been a great mimic and had made him laugh as they'd sat round the campfire melting marshmallows on sticks. Before that he hadn't laughed in a while. He had only ever seen her once again, years later when he'd gone to a sociology conference at New York University. They'd met in a bar in TriBeCa. She was tall and angular with big raw hands and an equine face that made him think of Virginia Woolf. No doubt she would have liked that association as she was trying to be a writer, but without much obvious success. She'd been married for a while to one of her Latino students from the literacy class she taught once a week to make ends meet. But it hadn't worked out.

There had, Adam thought, been something a little down-at-heel about her, a little desperate. He had bought her dinner, feeling slightly overwhelmed by the details of her chaotic life and been secretly relieved when the evening was over. He had not seen her since, but they'd kept in touch, tied by their childhood summer, she extending a permanent invitation to repay the dinner if he was ever back on her side of the Pond. She always sent Christmas cards. One had mentioned that she had published a story in the *Atlantic Monthly*. He was genuinely pleased and sent a postcard congratulating her; in fact, whenever he was away, he would usually drop her a card; a Velázquez from the Prado, a Minoan figurine from Crete. While in Paris he had sent her one of the Rothkos mentioning that there was someone new in his life. Her next Christmas greeting, in her familiar looping American script, had generously included them both: 'To dear Adam and Maggie.'

∾

It had been those words that had so hurt her. Their names linked together on the inside of the card, a tasteful photograph of a fir tree, its boughs bent with crystals of snow, wishing them *Season's Greetings*. It had made her cry, that acknowledgement of them as a couple, an item. But it had come too late. Five days before Christmas Adam had told her he was moving out.

'Maggie, I can't do this anymore. I just can't give you what you want.'

'I don't understand. I don't know what I've done. Anyway I've never told you what I want.'

'You haven't *done* anything. It's probably selfish, but I need more space. I need to be in my own place, have time to get on with my next book. I'm sorry; really I am that it hasn't worked out between us.'

Perhaps she should have seen it coming. But she hadn't. She had thought that now they had found each other they would grow old together. How many more chances did one have of happiness on the slow slide down towards fifty? As far as she was concerned, there was nothing much wrong. Nothing that couldn't be negotiated, sorted out through talking and a bit of gentle, mutual care. But that was just the trouble. He wouldn't talk. Not about feelings anyway. She remembered how, when in bed one night as she had lain with her back against the curve of his stomach, his face buried in her hair like two spoons in a drawer, how he had mumbled something about the vicar's words being, all those years before, just a formula, how he'd never even met his mother, and that he could have been talking about anyone. When she had tried to probe, to draw him out, he'd just clammed up, saying there was no point in talking about it. When he'd told her he was leaving she had suggested Relate, but she had known in her heart that he would never agree to go. 'Maggie, that's *your* solution. I don't do therapy; I don't even accept it as a paradigm.'

She hadn't meant to love him. When they'd first met that day, by chance, in the bookshop in the Festival Hall, she hadn't been particularly attracted to him. They'd both been killing time. He had been waiting for his train from Waterloo, while she, too early for her appointment with the design company for whom she did the occasional watercolour for their greeting card range, had been idly checking the racks to see if they stocked any of her designs and had accidentally knocked over a pile of books with her portfolio. He had helped her re-stack them. She had thanked him, perhaps rather too profusely, and they'd ended up going for a coffee. He had asked about her work and something in the tone of his voice, some slightly forced air of interested politeness, had made her wonder if she had sounded dismissive or rude. She had not meant to be. She knew she could appear either too opinionated or too shy. People who didn't know her thought her feisty. She alternated between feeling wary and prattling on, wanting to say something interesting or wondering if she was just sounding pretentious. She knew her unease made her self conscious. Nevertheless, he'd asked for her number and the following week had rung her. Suddenly he was just part of her life.

'I'm not in love with him,' she'd told her friends, 'after all he doesn't know a thing about art. How could I possibly be in love with a man who doesn't know his Picabia from his Pollocks? Seriously though, it just sort of works.

He's nice and likes Suzie; I like his sons. We have fun and I fancy him.'

And now, now after two years, after he had woven himself into the fabric of her life, he had suddenly snipped the stitches, cut and run. He seemed to have done it so easily so that now she was left feeling like a piece of old knitting, the unravelled thread all twisted and furred. She no longer knew whether the man she'd been with for two years was the real person or this cold stranger who seemed to have dropped a steel portcullis in his head leaving her stranded on the other side. She hadn't known she would miss him so much; his skin next to hers, the fur of his stomach against her spine, even his snoring. Perhaps you never recognised love for what it was until it was no longer there for the taking.

For an intelligent man, he was so disconnected from his feelings. She'd tried to pinpoint when it had started, the shift, the slow, imperceptible withdrawal that only now she could begin to chart. Perhaps it had been when he'd agreed to help set up a new course at Newcastle. He'd get up at first light, leaving her sleeping, to catch the earliest possible train and then not phone all week, caught up with his own agenda in the department.

'Maggie, why all the fuss? You know I'll be back at the weekend. What is there to say? You know where I am. You know what I am doing. Honestly, you really don't understand the pressure of academic life. You'll still be there when I'm back on Friday, but my paper has to be in.'

She had begun to feel pushed to the margins of his life, as if she was simply filling in the gaps between more important events like that Styrofoam packaging used to send fragile objects through the post. All she wanted was to matter. Was that too much? It had seemed so. Perhaps intellectual intelligence was the last refuge of the emotionally damaged. Work appeared to be the only place where he felt really in control. It was a known quantity. She remembered that night just before he had moved in, how in her cold dark kitchen he'd lifted her skirt and, pushing her hips hard up against the edge of the cold steel draining board, had entered her with an urgent insistence and then, quite suddenly, burst into tears. He had said it was for all the wasted years with Joanna; for his inability to resist her histrionics and emotional blackmail. Perhaps that was the moment Maggie had started to care. Vulnerability was, after all, erotic. She had held his face close in the dark and tried to comfort him, wondering, as they had stood in the puddle of shed clothes, if this was the first time that he'd wept since he'd been a child; if his tears, as his mouth had reached, wet and hungry for hers, were really those of a young boy for his dead mother.

Maybe that was the key to his leaving, maybe excessive childhood suffering had made him cruel because it had left him unduly self-protective, unable to empathise with what she had come to feel for him; this unromantic, daily sort of love.

They had gone to the cinema the night he'd got back from Newcastle. She had known there was something wrong when she had tried to slip her hand into his and he'd withdrawn it. That small movement had felt like a blow in the chest.

[9]

'Why did you do that?'

'Do what?'

'Move your hand.'

'I didn't. You're imagining it. I was just getting comfortable.'

She had, for sometime now, had the feeling that things were out of kilter, that there was something she should know about that she couldn't even name. The next evening she had cooked *spaghetti vongole*, a favourite of his, laid the table with candles, placing each fork and napkin with great precision as if by making everything perfect she could safeguard herself in someway. As they had sat working their way though a bottle of Rioja she had known she had to ask him.

'Adam, are you going to leave me?'

It had been then that he admitted it, that something had changed, that he just didn't feel the same anymore. 'I'm sorry Maggie.' It was as though he had been waiting for her to force his confession.

He'd gone straight upstairs and thrown his things into a holdall. 'I'll pick the rest up some other time. There's not much. Just a few books.' But she'd known he would never come to get them.

She hadn't wanted to cry or to make a fuss, to mirror Joanna's manipulative behaviour, but the tears had come anyway, silent, unbidden, streaming down her face as she had stood on the doorstep watching him load the car in the icy evening air. All along the street, lights from newly decorated Christmas trees blinked in the brightly lit windows.

'Now you are going I can say what I've never dared to say before,' she'd said looking him straight in the face, 'that I learnt to love you.'

After that she had turned quickly into the house, not waiting to watch him get in the car and drive away, shutting the door against his loss and the winter dark.

∼

Belle's apartment was above a Chinese restaurant on the Lower East Side, a tiny oriental island in the once largely Jewish neighbourhood. Whilst some of the old sweat shops and tenement buildings with their heavy iron fire escapes had been taken over by young artists, or turned into Tarot reading or tattoo parlours, there was nothing hip about The Lotus Garden with its murky interior, its cheap red lanterns and lurid gilt frames containing day-glo Chinese dragons. The stairway leading from the side door up to Belle's apartment smelt of cats and boiled washing. The visit had been a sudden decision. When the Christmas card with the snow-laden pine branches had arrived, Maggie had, on the spur of the moment, phoned Belle. She needed to get away, put some distance between the sense of rejection and confusion Adam's leaving had stirred in her, and Belle had seemed genuinely pleased.

'Come any time. Anytime you like, Maggie, I'd be delighted to meet you. I can't believe we have never met before. I've nothing planned, no commitments. I'm so sorry about Adam. He's an idiot. He never struck me as very in touch with himself. That summer we spent together as children, he never once mentioned his mother and he'd only lost her three months before. To me that didn't seem quite normal. But I just assumed it was his English stiff upper lip. And honestly he hadn't seemed to have changed that much last time I saw him. Maybe that hurt just went very deep. I don't know. But men! Seems they're just as useless both sides of the Atlantic. There certainly aren't any here worth having!'

Her apartment consisted of three interlocking rooms: a living room with an old floral sofa covered in cats' hairs, Belle's bedroom, and a room with an old wardrobe, its bursting doors tied together with string, a cat litter tray full of chalky cat turds, and a broken filing cabinet. In the kitchen the table was barely visible under the piles of old newspapers, the bits of photocopying and the latest batch of unmarked student assignments. At the very end was a tiny bathroom. It had lost most of its tiles and from the hairline crack in the sink, which ran from tap to tap, water seeped slowly onto the floor.

'Hope you don't mind cats. I used to have mice,' Belle said taking off her heavy tweed coat and slinging it on the nearest chair.

'Not at all,' Maggie answered, handing her the flowers she'd bought at the airport florist. She hoped there weren't also cockroaches.

≈

When Belle wasn't teaching she spent most of her days at her chaotic kitchen table, surrounded by piles of washing up, correcting and sending out stories to various literary magazines. She'd won a couple of prizes in contests and was waiting for her luck to change. But this week she had to teach most days. She taught a literacy class out in a small college in Brooklyn. Maggie admired her gritty tenacity for she hated the journey, and hated the students who were mostly not interested in learning at all.

'I also hate, Maggie, that last term I slept with the guy who teaches Math. After a few weeks he told me he needed to get away and have some time to think things through; that he wasn't sure he was over his last relationship and thought he was still in love with his previous girlfriend. I feel awkward being around him now, but I have to go, I need the money.'

≈

As she came out of the subway on 68th Street Maggie turned up her coat collar and walked towards 70th Street. The sky was heavy with snow. It was much colder here than in London, the sort of cold that got into your bones, weather straight down from Canada and off the Great Lakes with no Gulf Stream to warm it up, she thought, as she walked west towards Central Park. She had always wanted to visit the Frick with its Rembrandts and El Grecos. She particularly wanted to see Vermeer's *Officer and Laughing Girl*. She'd do the smaller galleries in SoHo and Chelsea on Monday and Tuesday and leave MoMA until her last day. The Frick was more like a stately home than a museum with its elegant, serene rooms built in the

European style by the industrialist Henry Clay Frick, in 1914. A luxurious, appropriate home for a successful industrialist and paterfamilias, it was a museum not only to art, but also to an ordered successful life. She particularly liked the enclosed courtyard garden with its marble fountain. Sitting there among the ferns listening to the trickle of water was like stepping into a Henry James' novel. She felt sad being there alone. All her recent trips abroad had been with Adam. She had got used to taking him round galleries, educating him about art. He had, for a while, at least, been a willing pupil. But now she had to find a new centre, make sense of this renewed single status. What was it that all those self-help manuals always talked about — loving yourself? Was that the key? She'd never thought that she would ever have to face being on her own again. Not at this age; she'd expected they would turn grey together.

~

When she climbed the cat-scented stairs to Belle's apartment, she found her with her arms plunged in the kitchen sink trying to make half-hearted inroads into the piles of washing-up. A wet pyramid of crockery, saucepans and glass was balanced on the draining board. As Belle went to fetch a cloth for Maggie to help her dry, the whole edifice slipped and a tumbler smashed onto the floor. 'Shit, goddam shit!' Belle exploded angrily, bending to pick up the broken glass and cutting her finger, which began to bleed profusely all over the floor. As Maggie handed Belle a cloth to staunch the cut, she noticed her face was streaked with smudged mascara and that her mouth was set in a tight little pucker. She'd been crying.

'The son of a bitch didn't even tell me,' Belle said shoving her bleeding finger angrily under the cold tap so that the blood swirled among the debris of coffee grouts and unwashed cups. 'I only learnt by chance. If I hadn't gotten to work there again this term, if I'd applied for another job, I might never've found out that he's getting married. Married! And he never even told me, the jerk. So I stood there in the staff room and threw a cup of coffee at him. Got him right in the groin. That caused a bit of a stir, I can tell you,' she sniffed.

'Belle come and sit down. How's the finger? Let me have a look. Do you need a bandage?'

'No, it's fine,' she said parking herself on the only free stool not covered by papers and wrapping the discoloured dishcloth in a wad around her damaged finger.

'Had you been with him long?'

'No, I wasn't with him at all, that's the point,' she said, brushing a strand of faded hair from her long damp face. Maggie noticed, for the first time, there were streaks of grey in it. 'He slept with me a couple of times and then made the excuse that he wasn't over his previous relationship and needed time to think. Think. Ugh! And now he's getting married. He didn't take long to think about that, did he?' and she started to cry again, hot, angry tears. 'At least I ruined his new trousers though. A direct hit right where it showed.'

'Was that a good idea?'

'Sure, it felt great. It was no more than he deserved, the lying sonofabitch. Maggie, the worst thing is that I now have to go back and teach there and listen to all that wedding shit. I can barely make ends meet. Not until the book is done and I sell it. Then it'll be different if I can just get it with the right publisher. Then I can put all this crap behind me. But at the moment I don't even have next month's rent. Married! I'd have married him if he'd asked. Why didn't he ask me?' her voice was wistful, hardly audible. 'Perhaps,' she said, her anger flaring again, 'because she's tiny, ten years younger than I am with long blond hair and has had a nose job and I'm 5' 10', my hands are too big and I look like a horse. But I don't look my age, do I Maggie? And we really did have something in common. What's it with me and men?' she asked her face beginning to crumple again, 'they never last more than a couple of dates.'

∼

Fifth Avenue. Maggie turned up past the Flatiron Building from E23rd Street towards MoMA. It was still cold, though the sky had cleared and was now high and icy blue. She was glad that Belle had gone to work early, glad to get out of the apartment. She didn't want to be ungrateful, it was generous of Belle to have her to stay, but she felt as if she was drowning. She could hardly cope with her own hurt let alone Belle's. Waking early, she had crept from her mattress on the floor in the corner of the front room and tiptoed across the chaotic kitchen for a pee with a sinking heart. But she genuinely loved Belle and one afternoon, when she was out, Maggie tried to clean up a little, hoping that it would help Belle feel cared for. She had bought a bottle of wine and a pot plant, which she'd thought might cheer her up. She had washed the floor, done the washing up and placed the begonia on the kitchen table. But Belle had been upset and had accused her of moving her things. Maggie had not intended it but perhaps her domesticity had felt like a tactless reproach. She began to feel the place closing in on her, her mood slipping.

She walked briskly because of the cold and because it was her last day and she had to make the most of it. Tomorrow she would be going back to London and have to face up to the reality of life without Adam. This trip had just been a diversion. She wondered what it would have been like to have been here with him. He had always meant to introduce her to Belle. They'd often talked of coming to New York together, perhaps when he'd next had a conference. It was his sort of city. He liked the downtown bars, the style and energy. They would have had fun. He liked eating out, drinking, having a good time. On her own she was much more frugal. That's what she'd learnt to love about him, the way he balanced her life. She was too introverted. All those years working in her small studio at home doing watercolours of peonies and cherries for card companies had taken their toll. She could spend days without seeing anyone now Suzie was away at college. He was the opposite, extrovert, sociable. Yin to her yang, she thought sadly.

She spent a long time looking at the Americans. She was drawn to Barnett Newman's austere monochromatic canvases, his mystical zips of paint that were supposed to represent heaven or at least a spiritual dimension. She loved the de Koonings, the Motherwells and Pollocks. All that pure expressionistic feeling poured onto the canvas, all that unmediated spontaneity and energy. She was so absorbed that it took her quite by surprise when she moved into the next gallery and there it was, suddenly in front of her, the deep crimson and magenta of the Rothko that had been on loan to the exhibition when they'd been in Paris. She started, taken aback, as if she'd just bumped into someone she hadn't expected to meet and a dry, involuntary sob caught in her throat.

And then it all came rushing back—his wet mouth on hers in that small, high Paris room; his fingers opening and reaching inside her, for somehow he had touched that lost, unnamed part of her, that hidden core behind the façade of professional designer and single mother. And she remembered how, after they had made love and the room darkened, she had lain with her head on his thigh stoking his long pubic hair, her fingers caressing the corrugated skin of his balls—like the ripple of hard sand after the tide had gone out—cupping them as she might hold walnuts gently in her palm. And she wondered how it might have been if they had been able to dare, and had stayed there together in that red vulnerable space, in a place of trust where he could shed tears for his dead mother and he had touched and known her, where she was neither mother nor painter, but simply herself.

Maybe that's what those moments had given her, she thought, standing in quiet contemplation in front of Rothko's stained red field of colour as the other visitors listened clamped behind headphones to the gallery commentary. Maybe that's how she could make sense of the pain of his leaving; that, for a second, he had given her a glimpse of a depth, of a hidden strength she didn't even know she had.

Yet still she wanted him. God how she wanted him; the touch of his skin, his warmth, his caustic humour. But no, she didn't need him. He had revealed to her, without even realising it, who she was and now, maybe if she was brave enough to embrace it, there might be some new role waiting for her when she got back to London. Some different turning she could take on the road up ahead.

MONA LISA

Molly's severed plait lay in her lap like something dead. She sat scowling into the water, a small girl clutching a pair of kitchen scissors in one hand and the ragged end of her hair in the other. She poked the centre of a nearby dandelion with the stainless steel points, and then angrily chopped the muddy crisp packet lying beside her on the path before jabbing the reflection grimacing back at her from the murky canal. After that she cut a hole in the knee of her jeans. 'Bugger, bugger, bugger,' she growled. 'Fuck, fuck, fuck,' she hissed, shocked at her use of the forbidden F-word.

There was no one else around. A cyclist had ridden past on the towpath and, in the distance, by the bridge, she could see a man fishing. Two drakes were pecking at some weed on the other side of the canal below the paint factory and, from the greasy water, the rusty skeleton of a pushchair poked through the film. She wondered if there'd been a baby in it when it had fallen in. Perhaps it was still lying on the muddy bottom, its little fingers clenched in a withered fist, its face bloated like a piece of grey bath sponge.

She examined the stub of her plait. It looked like the bristles of her Dad's shaving brush. When she'd been small she'd sat on the lavatory watching him shave in the morning. He used to get her breakfast before he went to work. It was always the same, Coco Pops with warm milk. He would try and get her to have muesli but she thought that it looked and tasted like rabbit food. In the evenings when he got home he would come in, take off his bike helmet and clips and then read to her in bed, before diving under the duvet hunting for her toes. 'This little piggy likes roast beef,' he'd growl from under the covers as she laughed and tried to escape.

She put down the scissors, shook her head and ran her free hand through her cropped hair. Her head felt light and unfamiliar like those dandelion puffs you blew on to tell the time. Perhaps it would simply float away now the rope of hair no longer weighed her down. She spread out her plait and thought of Arthur the cat. After he'd died he'd looked just the same for a while, soft and floppy, as if asleep. She'd gone with her Mum to look for a shoebox so they could bury him in the garden. But when they'd come back he had looked different; stiff and rigid, not like Arthur at all but something stuffed. His eyes had gone all white and milky. Her plait looked rather pathetic now, with its pink elastic bobble band tying up the thin end, so she coiled it up and put it in the pocket of her puffa jacket.

Really she should have been at school doing a spelling test. That's where her Mum thought she was. 'Have you got your lunch money?' was the last thing her Mum had said as she'd dropped her at the top of the road to turn left and walk the five hundred yards to St. Mark's Primary. After that her Mum would turn right to take Freddy to the child minder. But Molly hadn't turned left; instead she'd run straight on, right across the road squeezing through the hole in the fence that opened onto the bank above the canal. She'd half slid, half climbed down through the brambles littered with beer cans, cigarette packets and used condoms. Ugh, she thought, grownups are filthy. She'd been forbidden to come to the canal. She had had to promise after she had been here with Jake from the flats. Her mother had been beside herself. 'Molly I've been *frantic* where *have* you been? You must, never ever go there again. Promise,' she'd said as she'd shaken her by the shoulders and cried. She hated it when her Mum cried; she didn't know what she was supposed to do.

'Ok.' she'd said.

'No, I mean it. Say, I promise, Mum, I won't ever go to the canal again. Molly, are you listening? You're not listening. It's dangerous. Promise.'

'I promise.'

∼

Now she was here and had cut off her plait she couldn't really think of what to do next. She could cut her jacket, but that was new and she liked it. She wished she had bought some crisps with her lunch money. She couldn't go to school now; they would ask why she was so late and they'd already have done the spelling test and be onto their nature project on tadpoles. The tadpoles lived in a tank at the end of the classroom. They smelt. A funny earth smell mixed with a stink like the water from the bottom of the school toilets. They'd got the tadpoles from the Ecology Park. They'd collected them in a jam jar with some slimy weed and put them in the tank with stones. Their heads had got fatter and fatter and now they had little arms growing out of their sides. They looked like black jelly babies with wiggly legs. When they swam against the light you could see their insides. Wayne, who always sat with his hands down the front of his trousers when Miss wasn't looking, had asked her if she thought they'd pop if you squeezed them between your thumb and finger.

No, now she'd have to stay out the whole day, say she'd been ill and that her Mum had forgotten to write a note. Perhaps she should have come tomorrow instead because today they had swimming. She was in the school team and had a special blue badge. She'd been able to swim since she was three. Her Daddy had taught her in the sea near her Granny's house just below Golden Cap. That was in Dorset. She'd had a pair of red and white water wings which they'd bought at the beach shop where you could also buy ice creams and postcards, and he'd let them down very slowly without telling her, so that before she knew it she was swimming on her own. They'd gone to her Granny's in Dorset every summer before her Daddy had left. The little house had a garden with a long path and tall purple delphinium on either side and at the bottom there was a gate that led to the beach. There was also an old shed where her Granny kept deck chairs and a lawnmower that didn't work. Her Granny grew peas up sticks, which she helped her shell into a white enamel basin while sitting in the hammock.

Molly liked helping her Granny. Lamb with mint sauce and roast potatoes was her favourite lunch. Her Granny was a good cook. Her Mum never cooked that. Her Mum was vegetarian and bought lentils and dried beans from the health food shop where she was part of a co-operative. Molly hated lentils. Now she hardly went to Dorset any more because that Granny was the wrong Granny, her Dad's Mum.

Her Mum was useless. She messed everything up, it was all her fault. She was even scared of water and couldn't swim. 'Come on Lizzie, just lie back and float,' her father had said one summer. But her mother had spluttered and gone stiff, her arms beating against the waves like the wings of a frightened bird. 'No, honestly, I just can't, Jim. I'm going back to read my book,' she'd said turning back up the beach to sit on her towel behind the striped wind-break.

∼

Molly hadn't been to Golden Cap for ages. Moira didn't like it there. She always wanted to go to France. Moira was her Dad's special friend and she and her Dad would come and fetch her and Freddy in the Volvo and drive for two days until they got to a village in the hills. There was a swimming pool and croissants for breakfast and her Dad drank wine even at lunch time as well as supper, but it wasn't the same as Golden Cap. Anyway she hated Moira. 'Come on Molly, come to the village and help me buy the bread,' she'd say, or 'that's a really nice T-shirt you've got on Molly, pink really suits you.' That's when she hated Moira most, when she tried to suck up to her in front of her Dad with that funny smile of hers so you could never tell what she was really thinking. She didn't know who she hated most, Moira or her Mum.

She thought about how worried her Mum would be if she found out that she wasn't in school, but because she didn't know, she would be sitting stamping books in and out of the library as if it were just any old day. Molly quite liked the idea of her Mum being worried. She was fed up with her. 'Molly can you make Freddy's toast', or 'Molly just help me put away the shopping away, will you, I'm done in.' Sometimes when she went for a wee in the night she could hear her arguing with her Dad on the phone. 'I don't care what Moira thinks, damn it, Jim, they're not her bloody children.' The next day her Mum would be all snappy.

Once she'd found her at the top of the stairs crying. Another time she'd caught her in the bathroom about to take a load of pills. When Molly walked in she had pretended she'd shaken too many out of the bottle. Well, it was her own fault. If she hadn't gone on at Dad all the time, if she'd been more like she used to be before Freddy was born, then he would never have left. 'Pudding, I'm sorry,' he had said when he'd told Molly he was leaving; 'you know I'll always be your Daddy, whatever happens.' But she could see his point, after all Moira was far prettier and younger than her Mum. Just then a swan skidded onto the water in front of her, lowering its wings like an aeroplane coming in to land. She threw a stone at it and it turned and hissed at her.

∼

'It's quite natural,' Dr. Berg had said, 'feeling angry, blaming yourself. Lots of children feel like that. But no one's blaming you, Molly for what happened. Grown ups get things wrong too.' She hadn't wanted to go and see Dr. Berg and had sat beside the Ladybird books and torn comics in the waiting area with her arms folded, refusing to speak. In the consulting room she had only grunted one-word answers as she'd knotted and unknotted the end of her plait.

'Molly, please answer Dr. Berg,' her mother had begged. But she'd said nothing.

On the bus home she'd sat with her face bunched into a scowl looking out of the window.

'Molly?'

'I told you I didn't want to go. But you wouldn't listen. Dad wouldn't have made me. He *wouldn't*. I don't want to talk.'

∼

She got up and wandered along the canal. She should have bought some bread for the ducks. She tore up a bunch of short grass and threw it towards them. A couple swam towards her, pecked at it and then floated off. A man in a purple shell suit with a whippet on a chain lead said hello. She said hello back and he stopped and let her pat the dog. He had a tattoo on his arm of a rose. Underneath it said *Rita*. As Molly stroked the dog it quivered as if there were ants under its skin. It had an arched back and a long narrow head and its ribs stuck out as if it was starving.

'It's very thin.'

'That's the breed, love. They're bred light for racing.'

She wondered if she should be talking to the man, but as he hadn't offered her any sweets she presumed it was OK.

'What's its name?'

'Mona Lisa'

'What?'

'It's a famous painting, love. Of a lady with a funny smile. You can't tell what's she's thinking. Just like this one here,' he nodded indicating the dog.

'What you doing down here anyway? Shouldn't you be at school?'

'Not today. I'm waiting for a friend,' she lied.

~

She was sorry now she was missing swimming. She'd just started the classes for her bronze life saving medal. They used a plastic dummy instead of a real person. They had to rescue it and then give it the kiss of life by holding its nose and breathing into the hole of its plastic mouth. She wondered what it would be like if you couldn't swim, to know if you fell into a river that your lungs would slowly fill up like two plastic bags until you drowned.

She thought of her mother's flapping bird arms when her father had tried to teach her to swim, how she had spluttered and choked instead of blowing out when the salt water had got up her nose. She wondered what would happen if her mother was sitting here now beside her on the edge of the canal and by chance slipped and fell in. She could see her dark eyes opening in disbelief as she floundered, her legs dangling like the tendrils of a jelly fish, her white arms thrashing. Molly had been shown how to clamp the face of a drowning person and keep their head above water so the air passages stayed clear. She stared down into the murky depths from the bench where she'd parked herself and imagined her mother's frightened face, her mouth opening and closing, as she took in great gulps of filthy water. She saw herself ripping off her puffa jacket and jeans, then slipping quickly into the muddy canal and swimming towards her mother whose short dark hair was draped with weed like a helmet, her frightened fingers clawing at the petrol coloured water.

'Mum, it's OK, Mum, I'm coming.'

Then she imagined how she would grab her mother's head as she'd been taught in life saving, and then slowly, very slowly, push it down, down under the icy water until just a little jet of bubbles, like those from the shell of a boiling egg, gurgled from the corner of her mouth as she stared in terror and the canal closed over her head. She thought how pleased her Daddy would be that there'd be no more arguments on the phone, no more shouting when he brought her and Freddy home late on Sunday nights, how she would now be able to go and live with him. And how he would come into her room to say good-night to her as he had always done when she'd been little and read her a story and shout 'this little piggy loves roast beef' as he chased her under the duvet.

As she sat on the edge of the canal she turned her face to the sky and watched as the black clouds raced towards her from the other side of the city. Large grey drops splashed into the dirty water soaking her now cropped hair, which dripped in rats' tails down her thin white neck. She got up and unzipped her jacket, took off her sweatshirt, her wet jeans, her shoes and socks and huddled on the dirty verge among the dog shit and the cigarette butts, in her vest and knickers, digging her bare toes into the muddy grass.

She sat there for a long time, as the rain, a downpour now, washed over her small shivering body, until she couldn't tell whether it was the rain or her tears that were soaking her face.

JACKSON POLLOCK'S
CURTAINS

Bin liners and toilet rolls. We need toilet rolls. And fish? I could get some salmon and haddock to make a fish pie. Or skate? But he doesn't like skate, he says it's slimy and has too many bones. Yes, those'll do. Tiger prawns. On Special Offer. They'll keep in the freezer. And I need some milk, mustn't forget that. What else? Fruit. Potatoes? Something for dinner when the Humphreys come. Must remember Ken's jacket at the cleaners. It was ready yesterday afternoon. The ticket? What did I do with the ticket? Always losing things. Keys. Purse. In my other handbag. I left it in my other handbag yesterday. Milk. Mustn't forget milk. Cleaning liquid, polish and milk.

It's crowded. I don't like crowds. I should have come earlier. But that's good, no one can see in a crowd. You can't see pain. I wonder if there's anyone here I know.

Sheila? No, she said they were going to Sussex for the weekend. Simon's back from Brussels. Nice to have a weekend in the country. I love it at this time of year. The smell of the first hay, the cow parsley and ragged robin. I remember Grandpa's garden. The rhododendrons like pink pom-poms. We used to make them into earrings and crawl into the middle of the tangled bushes and take our milk and a packet of chocolate digestives we'd stolen from the larder. And picnics on the lawn; that's it. We had picnics on the lawn. Granny would lay out the big tartan rug under the lilac tree. We had cucumber sandwiches with the crusts cut off. I always remember Granny in a sunhat pruning roses. The garden had that lush midsummer green when everything is in full bloom; it's a much deeper green than in spring. Greensleeves. *Alas my love* . . . So English it makes me want to cry. But it's all nearly gone. Churches, cricket on village greens. Just nostalgia now. It was a lovely place for children to grow up. For a child. *Eeny, meeny, miney, mo* . . . It's not your turn. You have to stand in the queue and wait your turn. Not your turn this time any time spring time tralala time.

Do I need a trolley or just a basket? I didn't mean to come today, but I couldn't stay in the flat. And do what? Watch daytime TV? Kilroy-Silk and Oprah Winfrey; all those stupid people revealing their secrets in public. What am I supposed to do? Dust? It was spur of the moment and we do need a few things. I do need milk. It's full of antibodies. Breast is best. Breast, best, bestest.

I never could do Latin. But I liked Art. The highest grade Miss Crowther ever gave me was an A- for my Roman

Centurion. I copied him from *Romans in Britain*. Metal helmet, spear, leather cuirass—funny word that. Never mind. I won't need Latin to look for a little job. *Find a little job it will help you take your mind off . . .* A little teenie-weenie job, not too much . . . what was that song? *An itsy-bitsy teenie-weenie yellow polka-dot bikini . . .* a little itsy bitsy job. Nothing too demanding. Little by little. Slowly, now. It hurts. Oh God it hurts. It's coming. It's *c-o-m-i-n-g*. Pant now. That's a good girl. Time; you will feel better in time. Time's a great healer. Milk on her breath, her night-breath, starlight-breath. Alone, just the two of us; the rest of the world asleep. The hum-hum of the night-light and outside, in the dark sky, the Milky Way. *Catch a falling star and put it in your pocket save it for a rainy day . . .*

We sat and watched a shooting star through the high hospital window in that white room. My glass palace with walls of ice. Snow White. Cheeks like apples. She had cheeks like red apples. Worcesters, Coxs Braeburns. Poisoned? Did I? Did I? It hurt at first. The gush. Her gummy mouth hard and pulling. It's not soft like you imagine. But not anymore. All gone. *Poor Jenny's gone a weeping, a weeping on a bright summer's day.* Summer in the country among the long grass, red admirals in the current bushes. The leaves stank like cat piss.

Sheila grows currents but she's gone to the country for the weekend. Doing her garden. That's this year's project. Last year she did the pool. She only has the weekends. She wants to grow all her own veg. All organic—no pesticides, no poisons. Won't have to buy anything. She plans to take it all back to town. Courgettes—they have nice orange flowers. French beans and scarlet runners. Fill the freezer. Give some to friends. Planting seeds, pricking them out. Takes time for seeds to germinate deep in the wet dark earth. All those tiny shoots breaking from their leathery husks into a web of silky white threads. Days, weeks, months. Nine months. Lunar months. *Clair de Lune.* Moon-light. Moon-daisies. Moon-child. My moon-child, my shadow-child. You can see it moving on the screen. An elbow, a heel, a hand. Keeps you awake at night like indigestion.

I wonder if the Humphries eat fish. It's the first time I've done any real entertaining, the first time since . . . I could do pasta, I suppose but that's not grand enough and I'll have to make a pudding. Ken said it was important. *But only if you are sure, darling; only if you're up to it. Everyone understands.* But I must make a good impression. They're clients, after all. Must make an effort; can't just let myself go. Strawberry shortcake? Chocolate mousse? Too fattening. Have to get back my figure. Perhaps just cheese — a nice brie — and fruit? Fruit of the womb. Figs? Black on the outside soft and fleshy inside.

She was soft, her skin downy as a peach. My peach. My little girl. Nails like tiny oyster shells. We would have collected shells by the sea. Taken our nets and buckets and spades to the beach near Bottollack, with its tall chimneys, where the waves crash over the rocks and tin miners once worked in deep shafts under the sea, and looked for shrimps and starfish in the rock pools at low tide. Sand between the toes, in her hair at bath time. Drying her on my knee in a big white towel. Stories at bedtime. The Flopsy Bunnies, Mrs. Tiggywinkle.

Time they said. How long is time? This long, that long, too long. How much do you love me? Open your arms wide, wider and show me. This much, that much or t-h-i-s much? I love you *this* much. Only 49 hours. Such a little life. How many seconds is that? I can't work it out. I want to work it out. Now time goes on and on like a piece of elastic. Stretching and s-t-r-e-t-c-h-i-n-g. I didn't stretch. Something's wrong the obstetrician said. The heartbeat. The heartbreak. *Heartbreak Hotel. Only the l-o-n-ely dum, dum, di dum dum doo ah* . . .

I wish Ken hadn't had to go away this weekend. *You will be all right won't you darling?* Right as rain. The rain in Spain. Rain drops on roses and . . . I hate bloody Julie Andrews. All smiles and silly vowels. *You can always ring.* What does he really feel? Never quite sure. Always so apparently calm, so in control. He never really wanted . . . *Darling we are fine as we are aren't we? Just the two of us.*

Had to work on him, persuade him. Responsibility; I think he's frightened of that. He likes his freedom, his holidays, his job. I hated mine. Was glad to leave. All those skinny models with no tits. Obsessed with collagen and cellulite, with putting on half a pound. Who cares? Don't think he ever really felt the need, though you think he might have cared about his genes. Not like me. All the time that drumming getting louder and louder in my head. *It'll-soon-be-too-late, it'll-soon-be-too-late.* But I always wanted. Always. Remember Jonty and Joanna? One had blonde plaits, the other dark curls. They had real eye lashes and lids that closed and hand-painted mouths pursed into a tiny perpetual kiss. Six? Seven, I must have been then. We played hospitals in the orchard and had shoe boxes for beds, a washing up bowl for a bath and proper bandages. Granny made them each a dress with matching knickers. They had real pearl buttons down the front cut from her old blue evening dress. She cut it up, she didn't care. She'd worn it in Delhi at the Embassy Ball.

She used to tell us stories. How they slept on the verandah under mosquito nets, how she hardly saw her mother. They were called into the drawing room at six o'clock. Seen and not heard. Hair that had had a hundred strokes, faces all scrubbed. Had to curtsey. *Goodevening Mama. Goodevening Papa.* No school, just a governess. Deportment, French, Music and Art. She wore linen skirts, played tennis on the lawn outside the house in the evening. Her father shot a tiger once. It was a man-eater. Rare that. But once they've tasted human flesh they won't eat anything else. It terrorised the village; snatched a small boy, then a woman planting rice. Later grandpa had it in front of the fireplace in Eastbourne, but it had gone all crinkly like a crisp. I used to be frightened of its head when I was little, the glass eyes and sharp yellow teeth. Jonty and Joanna both had painted eyes. Periwinkle blue. I wonder where they are now? On the top shelf of some cupboard in a suitcase? That was a good game, hospitals. We had sticky plasters, real scissors and a tin of pink Germolene. I was happy then. I miss Granny, I wish she wasn't...

All right? Am I? I don't know. I suppose so. I wish Ken hadn't gone. But I didn't want to make a fuss; he's been so kind. I don't like the silence in the flat. I listen for sounds in the silence. I listen and listen. For what? There's nothing there. Don't be so silly THERE'S NOTHING THERE.

Concentrate or you will forget something. You should have written a list. Coffee. Yes, we'll need coffee after the meal. We've run out. Continental medium roast or Kenyan? I'll need milk for the coffee. The milk leaked. Can't cry over spilt milk. Little yellow patches of cholesterol leaked onto the pale blue flowers of my nightie. Smelt of sick when it dried. It wouldn't stop. Just went on and on. Seemed such a waste. They had to give me pills to dry it up. It seems the body just keeps going not matter what. Like clockwork. Tick-tock. Nails grow, too, after you're dead. Some women don't have any milk and have to use a bottle right from the start. Milk, hearts, kidneys. You can get them all at the supermarket. Spare parts; better than a hospital.

Everywhere I look there are pregnant women or toddlers in shopping trolleys at the checkout crying because they're not allowed crisps or sweets. They squawk and make a fuss when they can't have them. Mustn't make a fuss. No fuss. Good girl. There's a brave girl. I remember the sound of the radiators, all night in the pipes deep in the building gurgling and rumbling like a churning stomach. *Just the two of us.* Plp-plp. Plp-plp. Only the night-light, the star-light as if we were the only people in the world. You'd never guess at all those lifts and shafts, corridors, kitchens and laundries, all those levers and pulleys going round and round. Doctors, nurses, porters, radiographers, physiotherapists scurrying along like ants, like blood flowing through arteries. You can't see it. But if it stops . . .

For God's sake why doesn't she stop him screaming? He's got a packet of Smarties already. The terrible twos. Some people have no sense. No, don't do that, you silly cow, smacking won't help. Can't you see his little face?

I painted it pink because I knew; I'd seen her on the screen. She was tiny as a clenched fist, a floating shadow in a drift of snow; her eyes closed sucking her thumb, so peaceful and calm. Sheila teased me. Wait till you have your third it'll be all the old stuff recycled, none of this rushing out to buy overpriced little stripy jumpers from *Petit Bateau*. So pretty, so silly. I made the curtains myself to match the bedspread. They were covered in white rabbits. Everything was ready, folded, ironed and neat. *Please leave all empty trolleys here.* Yes, it's empty now; quite empty.

I should have made a list, and then you only buy what you need and don't shop on impulse. It's better to make lists, and then you can remember.

They said *come on dear and hold her now. You'll want to remember.* No, I don't. I don't. *One day you will.* I really don't. *Come on be brave, it'll help, honestly it will.* Please just like me forget, I just want to forget. Oh my poor darling. Her bloom all gone. All wrong. Sort of waxy. So cold and still. She needs more blankets. Hold her close, close, close. Warm her up.

A special room. The curtains like abstract paintings.
What's his name? All squiggly black lines and spilt paint.
It bothered me. I remember it bothered me that I could-
n't remember his name. Pollock. That's it. Jackson
Pollock. I saw a film once of him painting. He looked like
a dancer dribbling his pots of paint over his canvas.
Jackson. That's a strange name for a baby. An artist's
name, but they wouldn't have known when he was born
that that would be the case, that it would suit. We hadn't
chosen. We couldn't decide. We had a list. His and mine.
We never agreed. Said we would choose one when we got
home, let her grow into it. A name I mean. Too late. We
left it too late, she never did have . . . . Only for the certifi-
cate. Mary, like the mother of Jesus.

It's too crowded. I shouldn't have come. I can't breath.
Remember r-e-l-a-x. Breathe, slowly and deeply; that's
right, then you won't feel the pain. Ken got me to practice in the evenings. I'd lie on the floor on the Turkish rug
with my head in his lap, pretending, while he read the *FT*
and sipped his whisky. I'd lie there counting and panting.
You'd think you'd know what it was going to be like, but
you don't. What now, Ken? What do I do now? *Short doggy
breaths.* Ugh-ugh-ugh. *Well done darling. You'll be all right won't
you?* Right as rain. *You seem so much better. It's rather important. They need a senior partner, a financial expert. If you are
really sure.* Sure I'm sure. *I'll ring you. You're wonderful. So
brave. Love you lots.*

It's just all that silence and pinkness that I can't bear.
Why on earth did I paint it pink? Not very politically
correct. I could have painted it mauve or yellow. Now I'm

in the pink; drowning in Germolene pink and white rabbits. White rabbits have pink eyes. Goodness I'd forgotten that. For my ninth birthday I had a white albino rabbit. It had long ears with a black rim like a pencil line round the edge but they were all pink inside. You could see the veins if you held him up to the light. I called him Bouncer.

Daddy built a pen at the bottom of the garden by the greenhouse where Mummy grew tomatoes. Red Gems, that's what she called them. They had long stems and grew up bamboo canes. I remember that special smell when she watered them in the early evening after a day of sun. The ones you buy never smell like that. In fact, they have no smell at all. They never see the earth, are simply grown under artificial light on white stuff like cotton wool. It has a special name. Hydroponics or something like that, I think. I loved that smell of newly watered earth.

Bouncer had sharp black claws that scratched. He was always trying to dig out of his run like those prisoners in that war time movie who escape by digging a tunnel. I forget what it's called. All the officers have very clipped vowels and smoke pipes. Bouncer was obsessed. Dig, dig, dig. He was quite fierce really, but he would sit still for me, his ears flat against his back when I stroked him, his nose twitching. He never did it for anyone else. One night he got out. I went down before school in my dressing gown and wellies to top us his bran but he'd gone. September? It must have been late September. There was an autumny smell and I remember the grass was damp and there were cobwebs in the Michaelmas daisies. I couldn't believe it. I looked everywhere. He had dug right through the wire. He never came back. He probably got eaten by a fox. Mummy made me come in and get ready for school. I cried and cried. Brave girl Grandpa said. If he doesn't come back, we'll get another one; we'll go to the shop and you can choose another Bouncer.

God, what a queue. Even at the Express till. It's always the same when you're in a hurry. Why am I in a hurry? Ken's away. Nothing much I need to get back for and there's all that horrible pink to contend with. Pink gin. I could buy a bottle of pink gin and get drunk. I wonder what makes it pink? Stop it now. You're just being really silly, you don't even like gin. Being silly won't help. Falling apart won't help. One step at a time. I must do everything one step at a time. The man in the front must be shopping for a year. Ten-packs of loo roll. He must have big cupboards. Funny the things people buy. He's got nothing to eat. Just a trolley full of dog food, beer and lavatory paper. I wonder if he lives alone? At least he has a dog . . . It's still only Friday and there's a whole weekend to get through. I do wish Ken hadn't gone. Maybe I'll phone Sheila . . .

Now that's not very responsible leaving a pram like that. I'd never, not alone like that in a supermarket. I'd keep it with me always. You never know, you can't be too careful; there are all sorts of funny people around. You read about it all the time. Just a peep then. It can't hurt. Look at it all quiet, all tucked up, eyes shut, bubbles at the edge of its mouth. Milk-breath, night-breath, just the two of us in that high white room. They really shouldn't leave it alone like this. Anything might . . . not pink but brown, dark and curly. Have I got enough milk? Everything's ready. Just pay for the shopping and then . . . I will have to be quick. No one's looking. Hands shaking. Girl at the till waiting. She's looking at me. Why's she looking at me? Oh it's not a £20, only a £10. I'm all fingers and thumbs.

Breathe, now breathe slowly. Doggy pants. You know how; you've practised. Ugh-ugh-ugh. It stops the pain. It's coming, it's c-o-m-i-n-g. Is that the right change? I don't know. Keep the receipt. Take it back if it's not right. You can take it back. It hurts. For God's sake, damn you, it fucking hurts. Still no one watching. That's it. Meant to be? Foot on brake. Click. Past the checkouts, past all these people. Just keep going. Finders keepers. No one is looking. Automatic door. *Keep your receipt and win a free holiday in Spain.* The rain in . . . I hate Julie Andrews. It's all ready. Have to change it to blue . . . *feelin' blue, you'd be too* . . . What will Ken say? He never really wanted. Not like me. *Just the two of us.* But it went on and on *it'll-soon-be-too-late* and I couldn't get it out of my head. Brave girl, Grandpa said. That's it. If he doesn't come back, we'll go to the shop and get another Bouncer.

THE MONARCH OF THE GLEN

A Louis XV *escritoire* is standing in the middle of the grimy south London street. From the back of a van, an array of brass fire tongs, coal scuttles and a rusted iron bedstead spill onto the pavement as if the contents of some unfortunate house had just been whipped up by a hurricane. It is already dawn and the wind is lifting and straining at the awnings of the stalls, snapping the canvas like the sails of a dinghy. While dark it's never so cold but the temperature has dropped as the sky lightens to a metallic grey.

Sara blows on her numb fingers and makes her way through the maze of trestles piled with silver teapots, candlesticks and tarnished Sheffield plate. She's already been out for an hour. The market is crowded. Pantechnicons from the continent stand around the square like wagons in a Sunday afternoon western ready to ward off a Red Indian attack. Her torch flashes across mounds of bric-a-brac lighting up a pile of porcelain dolls, their painted bisque faces staring dumbly into the cold dawn. Most have lost their hair and their bald lobotomised skulls look like boiled eggs with the tops sliced off.

> In loving memory of my baby brother, Joshua Ashford born 1803 died 1806. He lies with the angels. Not lost but gone before.

She picks up the yellowing hand-stitched sampler and shivers despite her thick layers. The cold has wormed its way in. She imagines tiny blue fingers forced in some freezing attic nursery, under the watchful eye of a governess, to execute the near invisible stitches and wonders at such sanctioned misery.

The market is a graveyard, the point where the flotsam of centuries comes to rest. Every Friday she follows the same routine. Alarm at 4.30; then the unwelcome glare of the electric light in which she dresses in thermal vest, tights and fingerless gloves; the mark of the professional, the battledress of the fray. A life not consciously chosen, but a freedom of sorts, and for that she is grateful.

Dead leaves and crisp packets swirl along the pavement. She has bought nothing yet and can feel the mounting panic, the need to find that first piece at the bottom of an old biscuit tin—a Whitby jet necklace, a Georgian mourning ring or a mother of pearl needle case—and make the first fifty quid. It's always an act of faith. If she is five minutes late the other dealers will be there already, like jackals scavenging on the carcass of the past, the scent of profit in their nostrils, and she won't get a look in. When she was starting out she'd tried to buy in some of the smaller auction houses but could never quite get the hang of it, had never felt part of the club. She was always terrified of biding too much, of getting run up by the Ring because she was new to the Rooms and a woman. She knew that if they wanted to they would simply close ranks and cut her out. She had seen the same dealers at a number of sales, lurking at the back of the dingy rooms in their dirty anoraks, scratching their noses or pulling their ear lobes to register a bid with the auctioneer. Often the bids would only reach just above the reserve and she would see them later, a tight little huddle in some greasy spoon café round the corner, pulling a silver Georgian creamer or an early Victorian rose diamond ring from a deep pocket of a sheep skin jacket, when it would to be passed round among the bottles of HP sauce and the thick mugs of dark brown tea, to be knocked out to the highest bidder.

She feels pulled and thin, overstretched like old elastic. A pile of mirrors and frames is waiting in the studio to be re-gilded. That's what she really enjoys, using her hands. That's what she's good at, stripping back the centuries of dirt down to the original wood and plaster to reveal roses or fauns under her wire brush. She likes the crumbling delicacy of the gold leaf sheets, each lying like a medieval relic in its bed of white tissue. But it's slow work. She can't make enough to support the kids, but at least it keeps her sane and she won't ask Graham for more money. She won't go back to court.

'For God's sake, Sara, they don't have to have piano lessons and go to ballet. They're not going to grow up deprived if you let them give up,' her friend Monica cajoles as they sip Pinot Grigio at her kitchen table after the children's Monday evening gym. 'It's you who can't let go of the trappings of middle class life. You know Kirsty hates the piano and Lucy, well come on, you've said it yourself, is like a fairy elephant with two left feet and as likely to make a swan in the back line of the *corps de ballet* as she is to be a policeman. Why don't you just let them give up? They'd much prefer to be out riding their bikes.' And she knows that her friend is right, that not only would it save money, but also end the temper tantrums she has to endure whenever she mentions piano practice and scales.

'Guilt, I suppose, compensation for not being one of those mothers who is always ready and waiting at the school gates to hear about the delights of frog spawn. Monica, I'm always the one who's late, whose car is parked on a yellow line. The kids hate it when they're left waiting till last in the playground. They can be so moralistic. Some of those other mothers seem to do nothing but sit on fundraising committees and ferry their children between junior yoga and recorders. I know I shouldn't care, but it makes me feel as though it's all my fault.'

'What is?'

'I don't know. Everything. That they're growing up without a father, that I'll be the cause of them hating classical music. Just everything.'

Or was it guilt for demanding her own life when she could shut herself away in her studio listening to music among the pots of glue, the workbench with its neat row of saws and chisels, where she could use her hands and create something tangible? Restoration nourished her. To re-store. What was it she was storing, squirreling away? Ballast against the hard times? But she couldn't go back, not now, to those PTA coffee mornings, to the school run. She'd never been cut out to be a country solicitor's wife, had never *meant* to be one.

She had simply married the wrong brother. Perhaps if she'd had the courage to wait for Steve to settle, to return from his Venezuelan field trip, had not needed the assurance of his presence to show her that he cared, then she would never have given in and married Graham. Dependable Graham who had his entire life mapped out: a Georgian house with a gravel drive and room for two cars, a wife and a couple of children, then a partnership with Johnson, Grieves & Johnson. One evening in bed, as she was finishing the new Ian McEwan, and he was sitting reading his case notes propped against the pillows in their elegant bedroom, she'd looked up from her book and asked, 'Graham, are you happy? I mean *really* happy? Tell me what do you honestly want from life? I mean deep in your soul?' And he'd answered, peering over his glasses that if she could tell him whereabouts his soul was supposed to reside then he might be able to consider giving her a rational answer, but as presumably she couldn't, he wasn't able to oblige.

She stops in front of the baked potato stand. The potato is warm in her hands, earthy and reassuring. It is light now as she hunts up and down the rows of stalls full of Victorian clothes, old croquette sets and chipped Crown Derby, picking at the potato in its bed of tin foil.

It catches her eye by chance. There is something in their expressions that makes her stop. The frame is ugly, made of stained ash with copper, art nouveau swirls, found, no doubt, in a car boot sale or a house clearance in Hastings or some other down-at-heel seaside town. They must have made a comic pair, like the fat lady and the little man on those saucy postcards. Perhaps others had whispered as much but their faded sepia faces are tinged with, what—relief? It is this that stops her. Her heart somehow touched, drawn back across nearly a century.

There they stand side by side on their wedding day. A certain status at last. No more pitying looks or flushed cheeks when she's addressed as 'Miss'. Now she'd have a house of her own, a kitchen to keep, her own little brass knick-knacks to polish. Ironing and mending—sheets side to middle—make do and mend. There'd not be much money, but she would have a position. She'd be a house-wife, not just her father's drudge.

She had cared for him like a wife since she was fifteen when her flame-haired mother had died of bronchial pneumonia. She hadn't questioned it. It had been her duty. She remembered him as he was when she'd been little, dressed in his blue uniform, his moustache waxed into sharp points, his brass buttons polished and gleaming and the wick of his station lantern neatly trimmed. He would stand with his back to the grate, his boots polished, rolling a cigarette beneath the framed copy of Landseer's *The Monarch of the Glen*. She could still remember the smell of the shredded tobacco that he teased out into the thin white paper. Her parents had bought the cheap print in a second hand shop on their honeymoon. They had had no money, but her mother had persuaded him. 'Oh, go on, Doug. We need something over that mantle. It'll give the room a touch of class.' They had never bought anything before except a bed and a table but he had loved her so much that he'd have done anything she asked and handed over a week's wages. They had carried it back from Skegness wrapped in newspaper and string anxious not to break the glass, and he'd climbed onto a stool in his stocking feet, banging a nail into the wall above the fireplace, while she'd stood watching him straighten the varnished frame.

To his daughter he'd seemed invincible, like a god. His word was law. She wanted to please him, but was always a little afraid. She knew she didn't have her mother's grace or her neat figure, that their only likeness was her inherited red hair. She was, like him, solid and bulky, where her mother had been light and lithe. He'd never been able to forgive her for being a travesty of the wife he had lost. His anger had flared unpredictably if she dripped his tea in the saucer or forgot to have his slippers warming by the fire and he was slightly repelled by her big raw hands. After the funeral they had hardly spoken for weeks, the heavy blinds drawn against the daylight, trapping them in their silent grief. She had become used to moving around him like a wraith. He said little. So long as when he opened his chest of drawers he found his shirts starched and ironed, and there was cold meat and pickle waiting for him on the table, he'd leave her be. But, occasionally, he wasn't able to prevent himself from letting slip a wounding sarcasm.

The girl was all fingers and thumbs.

At eighteen she had joined the local choir. He'd been silent, grudging, but had said nothing if she laid out his tea before she left for her Sunday afternoon practice. She felt a certain unaccustomed lightness hearing her voice rise and mingle with the other voices lifting towards the vaulted stone arches. And there had been a lad, a farm labourer from the next village with slate grey eyes and dark brows. One day, as she'd been standing at the vestry door doing up the top button of her coat against the certain rain, he'd told her that she had a lovely voice, and they had walked back together across the water mead-ows where green cress grew beneath the hump-backed bridge.

They had talked. Rather he'd talked and she had listened, entranced. He wanted to leave the farm, to write songs and sing them in the music halls of the big towns. There was a call for tenors. He dreamt of Exeter, Bristol, even London. 'Think of it, Fred Bowers' name up in lights in Hackney or Islington.' That'd been his dream. After that he walked with her most Sundays. With him, for the first time, she felt almost graceful. But when she hurried home, her hair wet from a sudden summer downpour, her father had made pointed remarks about her mooning around after village lads. The boy had a reputation. Didn't she, foolish girl, know that? Types like him weren't interested in girls like her. He wouldn't have some hired farm hand making free with his daughter.

What would people say? He was the stationmaster.

She didn't argue. She didn't have the strength. She just stopped seeing him and then heard that he'd gone away. Her father had probably been right. What could a boy with eyes like that see in a girl like her? Now after choir practice she would come straight home and iron the damp washing airing in the scullery while her father smoked or read the *Railway Times* in the front parlour supping his Sunday ale. But she still had the daisy chain Fred had made one Sunday afternoon when they'd climbed to the top of the long barrow and sat in the tall grass looking out across three counties. It lay withered and yellowing on a nest of cotton wool in the secret drawer of her mother's little rosewood box where she kept her honey-coloured amber beads and the long pins that had held up her thick red curls.

She met Stanley Higgs through her father. He came to work as a clerk at the station. He called for her father every morning at seven to walk the quarter of a mile down the lane. Maybe it was because he was on the railways too, or perhaps because her father was getting old, becoming lonely with only her silent company, that he started asking the clerk to share a bite with them. He talked with her father about timetables, gauges, and the new level crossing as they ate the boiled beef and treacle pudding she had cooked, so that when Stanley invited her to accompany him to the church fête, her father merely grunted, knocking his thick stemmed pipe against the fender and scraping out the bowl with the end of a dead match.

She was thirty-two.

In three months they were married. She knew the village boys were sniggering behind the yew when she stepped out of church on his arm. Solid, bulky in her ivory crêpe, she stooped to hide the six inches she towered above Stanley's squat frame. But, laugh as they might, at least now they couldn't call her an old maid or shout 'spinster' behind her back as she came out of the village stores.

Sara takes a last bite of her baked potato and throws the greasy foil in the rubbish bin. She should move on, look for something to buy. The market is filling up with dealers and soon it'll be too late and anything worth having will have been snapped up. But the photo in its scratched frame continues to hold her.

'I'll take twenty-five quid,' the stallholder bids, clapping his hands against the cold. 'Nice bit of art and crafts, that. Worth that just for the frame.'

She looks up and realises he assumes she's considering buying it. The condition of the photograph isn't good. Small black dots fox the surface as if it has been thrown, for who knows how long, in some musty chest of drawers. Yet here they are more than ninety years on, at the end of the terrace, in front of their garden gate. Not to be pitied, but a part of the proper order of things.

The stout man looks uncomfortable. He is short and thick set, his neck sunk deep into his chest, the starched edges of his collar chafing his fleshy cheeks, his thick hair snaked in waves from the neat parting where a watered comb has recently left damp furrows. A silver chain and watch hang from his waistcoat button, straining across his broad midriff and a neatly folded white handkerchief pokes from his breast pocket. He looks as if he's borrowed the whole attire for the occasion. But he hasn't managed the shoes; he is wearing thick-soled working boots. Yet, there he stands, straight backed, proud, and apparently totally unaware of the spectacle that he and his timid, ample wife create.

She is clutching a spray of stiff ferns and waxy orchids and the lace trim on her crêpe dress hangs in folds across the solid abundance of her breasts. Sara wonders whether they even touched one another before their wedding day, this ill-assorted pair staring out at her across the decades, this quiet woman with her neat crimped hair and this stocky little man. Perhaps he had simply been fed up with living in railway digs, of coming home to bread and cheese every night. Maybe he had fallen in love with her spotted dick and the thought of tea hot and ready, set out on a clean cloth, when he got back from the station. Perhaps she had agreed to become his drudge instead of her father's—and her prize? The title 'Mrs.'

Had they done it on Saturday nights, conjugal rights by arrangement, his cold fingers reaching for her previously private places under the thick flannel nightie while she counted the creaks of the old iron bedstead as the paisley eiderdown heaved above her? Or maybe she just stared at the ceiling thinking of church the next day when she'd wear the new lilac gloves she'd bought in the Derby and Freeman's sale? They had been learning a new hymn. Would she manage the high notes, she wondered, dreaming of grey eyes and black brows, as the heavy shape above her rolled to one side and a sticky trickle ran down the inside of her thick white thigh?

It has begun to rain, a fine slow drizzle. Sara gets out her wallet. 'I'll give you fifteen quid for it. Look, you can see it's damaged.'

'Twenty smackers love and it's yours.'

She knows she'll never sell it, that it isn't worth the money, but she can't leave them here. She wants to protect them somehow, give them a home. Now she has to get on. She has bought nothing that will yield a profit and the electricity bill is still sitting on the dresser stuffed behind the school letter about nits. If she can't keep this side of her little business going she'll have to give up the restoration and the gilding and look for something nine-to-five, and that would be a real admission of defeat. She can hear Graham's hectoring voice condemning her irresponsibility and her infidelity.

'For God sake, Sara, I mean if you were so desperate to have it off with someone, did it have to be with my brother? You know he's completely useless, utterly immature. He'll never give up his research or playing at explorers. So you feel better do you, now that you've *expressed* yourself, explored your *soul*, broken up our marriage, the children's home, damaged their education?'

He had a point.

She wonders if she should just let Lucy give up ballet, because really she isn't any good at it. Perhaps Monica's right that she is only making her continue so that she doesn't feel as if she is depriving her daughter of the trappings of the life they've left behind? But it's easy for Monica to theorise from the safety of a thirty year marriage. It is six months now since she's heard from Steve. She isn't even sure where he is. Nepal? Bhutan? But then she hadn't expected it to be any different, even in those weeks when her body had come alive, when something damaged in her had been rekindled, restored to its natural balance by his touch, by his naked skin next to hers. She had loved him with every bit of herself as though he was embedded somehow in her entrails, but she had known that he had never felt the same. Was that because she had loved too much or because he could not love enough? Looking round the windblown stalls she wonders who had compromised most: her or the broad hipped woman in the stippled photograph, which of them had got the thin end of the wedge?

'Bought any thing?'

'Oh, Ginger you made me jump. No, nothing. Only one small frame and I shouldn't have bought that. Haven't even made my expenses. Have you got anything? One of my customers has asked me to look for some shell cameos.'

'Na, nothing you'd want, girl. This place is finished if you ask me. Germans and Japs have cleaned it out. By the way, Sara, you got a silver Fiesta? Better watch it darlin' 'cause when I went to move me van a bunch of wardens was sniffing round slapping on tickets.'

She shoves the frame in her bag and hurries through the stalls across the square towards her parked car where, as she turns the corner, a sycamore leaf blows across the pavement caught up by a little squall landing in front of a burley warden.

He is writing her a ticket.

She wants to scream that it's not fair, that she is doing her best; that the fine will be more than she has made all morning, but knows it will do no good and that she needs to move quickly before they tow her away. Then she won't even be able to pick the girls up from school. When people talked of freedom they never mentioned the loneliness, the exhaustion and responsibility. She thinks of the couple safely tucked in her bag and wonders if they'd been happy; if their lives had worked out, and if happiness was something you could simply decide upon and choose. And would she still make the same choices now, she wonders, ripping the parking ticket off the car, to have loved Steve and left Graham? Risk over certainty?

Still she didn't have time to think about that now.

MONDRIAN'S MOON

'I thought a geographer would be good at directions,' she says, winding down the window, turning off the ignition and giving him a big smile. He's waiting for her in the car park in shorts and deck shoes, dark glasses perched on top of his head holding back his curly grey hair. 'You left out a road, the bit that connects the motorway with the A4. I got terribly lost. The signs just sort of run out.'

The sun is pouring through the trees of the marina car park. It's very hot and the tarmac is shimmering. In places it has melted into sticky treacly pools. She steps out of the car careful not to get it on her flip flops or white trousers. She had taken a long time to decide what to wear, had changed twice. It was a boat, after all, so nothing too dressy. Jack had had a thing about boats, too, but in all the time she'd been with him, he'd never taken her sailing. Whenever she'd asked he had made her feel as though it was a synonym for commitment. 'Take me sailing, Jack, I'd love that. Come on,' she'd joke, 'I'm not asking you to marry me, just take me out in a boat.' But he never would. It had become a barometer of their relationship; his reluctance to yield to her in any way, to acquiesce to her simplest request.

She hadn't known which direction to take after she'd come off the motorway, hadn't even been sure that she was even driving the right way and not, in fact, heading back towards London. She'd had difficulty finding the turning, had taken the wrong right at the roundabout and then, when she'd driven the half mile down the narrow lane, there had been all that fiddling around punching in codes to open the heavy iron gate. Why all the protection? Did those living on boats have more to steal than those living in houses?

Getting lost had left her feeling anxious, like a rudderless ship. She'd forgotten to bring a map so only had his instructions to rely on which she'd hastily scribbled on the back of an envelope. It had been a whim, an impulse to come. She'd wanted to feel better, to stop caring about the situation with Jack that she could do nothing about. He was, Rod had told her when he'd phoned, going away the following week, but would love to see her again before he went. She was busy, she said, had to prepare for an exhibition. But then she'd lost confidence; maybe he wouldn't want to see her when he came back, would have forgotten her or found someone else. So she called. She could do tomorrow; but that was the only day. The rest of the week she had to be at the gallery.

Perhaps she should have kept him waiting. But she'd never been very good at holding out or playing games, dangling them on a string, keeping them interested. Even now at an age when she could no longer pretend to herself that she was still young, she was no better at it than she'd been at twenty. It had never gone away, this need, this desire. All the time she'd been with Jack she'd reigned herself in, afraid of asking for too much, so that in the end she had asked for nothing at all. Each time he'd left her, climbing out of their warm Sunday morning bed, kissing her on the cheek, she'd stood in her dressing gown on the doorstep beside the pot of shrivelled geraniums, wearing a fixed smile and holding back the urge to ask when she'd see him again. But he never said, never gave her that assurance, as if to do so would be to relinquish too much, give away some part of himself like those primitive tribesmen who thought if they were photographed they would lose a bit of their soul.

She wasn't a bad person. She'd battled and come through; had patched things up with her parents, made something of herself by going off to Saint Martins as a mature student and doing not very interesting jobs until she got her first show. Her children still spoke to her, having come through the difficulties of adolescence; she cared about her friends, remembered their birthdays, and gave a small monthly donation to Oxfam and *Médecins sans Frontiers*. But now that the kids were grown she realised that every time she lied about her age it sent her whole life out of kilter, dates skittering through the years like balls in a game of bagatelle. Nothing fitted anymore, the length of her marriage, the age of her children, whom, she realised, she was forcing to get younger with her. Yet, however tough life had been bringing them up alone, she'd always felt that if she worked hard, just hung on and had faith, that it would be alright in the end.

And now? Well now that the end was more nearly in sight, and the world, she realised, was not simply waiting for her to put in an appearance or be discovered, and that around the next corner there was not necessarily something gleaming and new, filled with promise or healing warmth, but another corner, the sharp angles of which had to be manoeuvred like all the others. One morning she had woken up and realised, just as one does when pulling back the curtains and noting whether the weather is cloudy or fine, that she'd reached the age when her choices had begun to run out.

That's why one evening she'd opened a bottle of wine, normally something she never did, for she didn't drink alone and hated the image of sadness that clung like a stain to solitary women drinkers of a certain age, and logged onto the internet. She'd been amazed at the variety of men. There were solicitors and architects, those in PR and finance, from the balding and bespectacled, to the tanned and the toned. Most of them were looking for younger women—even those who'd be lucky enough to find any woman at all—their profiles full of clichés behind which lurked, she was sure, their insecurities and failures, their foibles and their dreams. Yet the one word that was never used was love; as though what was being offered was only a bland replica of the real thing. And yet it was the search for this very balm that invisibly linked her to all these unknown men; this desire to feel special, needed, mirrored in the eyes of another. For it was as if all those who logged on in the small hours, alone in the silence of their rooms, the tossed covers of their empty beds gaping like an accusation, secretly knew that they had been expelled from a landscape where the sun eternally shines and the sky is always blue, knew that they'd somehow inadvertently fallen from the golden heights of coupledom into this grey limbo of singletons.

So this is where life had brought her, she thought, as she had rather half heartedly sent out her profile. I shouldn't have to be doing this. I should have been married for 30 years and be planning my children's weddings. Later she'd run herself a bath and lain back in the scented foam trying not to think too much about anything, letting the water grow tepid around her. Then, after she had dried herself and rubbed moisturiser into her hands and her feet, her stomach and her breasts, which despite everything were holding up quite well, she'd dressed in a clean white nightdress, one she never normally wore and had bought for an overnight stay in hospital, and climbed into her chaste bed, cleansed and anointed as a nun.

~

She'd been standing in a pair of knickers drying her hair when her daughter had come to ask to borrow the car.

'Why you getting all dressed up?'

'I'm going on a date.'

'Good for you.'

'I'm not so sure. I shouldn't have to be doing this. Not at my age. It's undignified.'

'Don't be silly, Mum. Smile. You look nice when you smile. Where's the key?'

'In my bag. Come and give me a hug and wish me luck. And promise not to drink.'

'I promise. And you'll be fine. You look great.'

As she'd stood in front of the mirror in her room, the voile curtains blowing through the open window on the warm summer air, she'd examined her naked body, the pale stretch marks like silver snail trails criss-crossing her stomach, the dark brown nipples. Would she pass? She was getting too old for this, for these endless new beginnings.

≈

When she'd first seen him across the bar, lounging on a sofa in a fresh white shirt, with a bottle of chilled champagne waiting in a bucket on the table, she knew it would be alight.

'Rod?'

So it could still happen, then, that tightening in the gut. She wasn't dead yet. He'd got up, kissed her and held her hand a moment longer than was necessary. She'd sat down beside him sinking back into the leather sofa. She was glad she'd taken care getting ready, knew that she looked OK. The conversation had gone pretty well. She couldn't remember what they'd talked about, for she was too aware of his tanned arm lying in its crisp white shirt sleeve on the back of the sofa just an inch from her bare shoulder. By the third glass of champagne he'd reached and brushed her hair from her eyes.

'You have a great smile,' he said.

She'd asked about his work. He worked for British Waterways regenerating the canals. That was something she could be interested in, she thought, if she made the effort. She listened, wanting to be attentive. She wasn't good at small talk, was much better with ideas. She missed Jack's iconoclastic wit. Not that he'd been too hot on ideas, but he had made her laugh. Still what was the point of thinking like that? He wasn't coming back. Commitment hadn't been his thing, he'd said, though he'd woken beside her regularly for 18 months; for Christmas, for her birthday, had emailed her daily, filled her weekends so that her kids hadn't needed to feel guilty that she was too much on her own. It had been enough for her to have ear-marked him a small but consistent space in her life. Then he'd just disappeared. She tried to get on with her life, to do what she would have advised her daughter to do in the circumstances. Eventually she had phoned him.

'Listen Rachel, the truth is I've met someone else. I know I should have told you.'

'Yes, you should have. You've been sleeping with me.'

'Look, there's just no point in going over it. There's nothing to be gained. What's done is done. I want to live with her. We can still be friends.'

'Live with her? You've only known her a few weeks. You've always said you don't do serious or commitment. I can't believe the cliché about us being friends.'

'I'm sorry.'

She'd put down the phone and howled then splashed cold water on her face. It was red and puffy. She looked hideous. Crying was only becoming in the young.

∽

In the bar the champagne had gone to her head. It was hot and she wasn't used to drinking in the afternoon and had eaten nothing.

'So tell me about your art,' Rod had said.

She'd been dreading that and the inevitable 'well what do you think of that Unmade Bed?' She'd recognised the slightly discordant note when she'd suggested that looking at a copy of a Monet—even a good one—and an actual Monet were not, as he insisted, the same thing.

'But why not if they look exactly alike? What's the difference? Why is one any better than the other? That's just snobbery.'

'It's not really about how they look,' she said softly, trying not to sound dogmatic, 'it's the fact that Monet had the idea and the person who did the copy, well, they just copied. Monet isn't just one painting but the sum of all his work, all his thinking. Anyway I'm not a painter. I'm a conceptual artist.'

'Well, you look like Francoise Hardy when you smile.'

~

The pubs were closing and crowds of teenagers milled in the streets in the thick night air wearing short skirts and cut-off T-shirts as if they were in the Mediterranean. She had gone with him to the Italian restaurant around the corner. They had eaten *spaghetti fungi* and been the last to leave the restaurant. At the end of the meal he'd leant over to kiss her. His mouth had tasted of cream and garlic. As he'd walked her to the bus stop hot air bounced off the dust-choked pavements of Upper Street.

'If you wait with me you'll miss your train.'

'I was hoping you were going to ask me back.'

'Not tonight, Josephine,' she'd laughed, giving him a quick kiss and running towards the No 4 bus.

~

He'd caught the last train with a couple of minutes to spare, though it had stopped at every station. 'Hope you're not stuck at Paddington,' she had texted. He'd texted back. 'Ring me.' 'I'm virtually asleep,' she'd replied. He could still smell her perfume on his skin. She certainly had a great mouth. He wished though, now, that they hadn't talked about Monet. He had been out of his depth, but had felt the need to insist, to push his point home even though he was unsure of his ground. The truth was he'd never been with a clever woman. Pretty women, capable women, but he'd always avoided the intellectual ones. He took the others for weekends to Paris and they'd spend an hour or two in the Louvre before getting down to the sex. Most of them knew nothing about art so were impressed, but he knew he was bullshiting, that he was all show and no substance.

Straightforward women like Katie were too predictable. That's why he had broken it off with her, wasn't it? Her compliance had begun to annoy him, the way she'd leave all the decisions to him, always acquiesce to his views. Surely he was capable of more than that? Why could she never make any decisions of her own? He should read more. He *would* read more. That's why he'd ended it because he wanted to ... what? Now he was not quite sure what it was that he had wanted. But with Katie he didn't have to stretch himself. He set the agenda. She just went with the flow, curling up beside him naked on the sofa in his old rugby sweater. She had a great body, knew how to look after herself, but there were things he wanted to do, things he couldn't do with her around.

The carriage was empty. He leant his head against the window and dozed, watching the moonlit summer wheat fields disappearing along the track one by one so that he could hardly tell which the real fields were or which their reflections mirrored in the train's cool glass.

Ever since Oxford he'd known there was another world he could enter if only he'd had the will. But he'd always avoided the gangly philosophers with their intense, slightly absurd existential talk, the poets with pasty faces and pigeon chests. Perhaps he'd been surprised to be there at all. After all he hadn't made it to Manchester Grammar. Cardinal Hume had been second division. Boys from his background didn't usually go to university. Not from an end of terrace like his. So he'd hunkered down into a world that relied on physical prowess, on being one of the crowd and had sat on the verandha of the boat house with a pint of Shires watching Teddy Hall take the head of the river in the May sun. Pretty girls, that's what he'd always gone for; straightforward, pliant and eager to please.

As he'd driven from the station back to the boathouse a fox had run in front of his car, the white tip of its bush erect in the moonlight. It was 2 o'clock when he got to bed and still hot, the air like dark velvet. He'd slept with the windows and the hatch doors open, naked, the cover thrown off, his body latticed by the shadows of the willows. He thought again about the Monet conversation and then remembered her smile, the way she'd looked at him from behind her curtain of auburn hair, challenging, quizzical, sad, not like a mature woman at all but like a girl of twenty. Is this what he wanted, something textured, raw and real; something with depth? In the dark he could feel her lying there beside him, the soft curve of her stomach, the arc of her hip as he felt himself stir and he slipped his hand down between his sticky thighs.

In the morning the sheets were wringing wet.

~

The next day she'd phoned Alicia. 'He looks nice and seems keen. He bought champagne, for godsake. How many men do that? But I hate it when they ask me about postmodernism and then resent me for explaining it, as though I'd personally invented it just to insult them or pull the wool over their eyes. I think they feel that I've dumped them in a foreign city and run off with the map. Maybe, Alicia, it's just too soon after Jack.'

'Come on, Rachel. Think how you've felt since Jack left, and it's not as though he knew much about art. Anyway, he treated you pretty shoddily. I don't know why you cared so much about him.'

'Because he made me laugh and he didn't give a shit that he didn't know about postmodernism or anything else. I prefer that. I hate it when they mind that they don't know and then get resentful when they ask me to explain, as if I'm trying to chop off their balls. Fuck it, Alicia, I'm an artist. I can't pretend I don't know or care about these things. What am I supposed to do? Bat my eyelids and discuss Match of the Day? He's charming, though and I fancy him.'

'Well, if you want my advice, I'd go for it. The world isn't full of desirable 50-something men. Find out what he's like in bed. Sorry, have to go. My next patient's due at half past. Speak soon.'

∼

She follows him along the duckboards. The marina is full of narrow boats. Some have flowers painted along the hulls and window boxes of geraniums. Others have bicycles tied to the roofs and full grown herb gardens that have been planted in old sinks. All are moored very close together and she can see people cooking supper or sitting out on deck enjoying the last of the evening sun.

His boat is by a bank of willows and yellow iris. A flotilla of swans glides past and a couple of Canadian geese peck at the water weed. It must be beautiful to wake here in the morning, the mist rising over the river and the sound of the dawn chorus. As he helps her on board she notices the silver hair poking from his open necked shirt. How different people's bodies are, like unexplored countries. You have to get to know their customs and ways before you can make sense of them. She wonders what it would be like to lay her head there and thinks, unwillingly and painfully, of Jack. So, she's already decided then? She's going to stay and not drive back to London.

Once inside the boat she's surprised. What had she expected, something slightly alternative, a bit hippy? But it's all pale wood, smoky glass and stainless steel like a smart hotel. There's champagne in a bucket, olives and dips. He takes them out onto the deck at the stern while she goes to the lavatory. When she lifts the lid there's a swirl of yellow in the bottom of the bowl. He's forgotten to pull the flush. In such a small space he can probably hear her peeing, so she turns on the tap.

Back outside he pours her a drink, and then breaks off lumps of bread, which he throws to the gathering swans. Why is it that swans manage what humans so often fail to do, to mate for life? She asks about him. He talks about his time at Oxford. How he wished, now, that he'd done PPE. He'd enjoyed Geography but sometimes he regretted that he'd not made more of his chances, had stuck so resolutely to the sporty crowd. 'We avoided the intellectuals, thought they were all a bit odd.'

'Well that's geographers for you!'

But he doesn't laugh, doesn't pick up the baton of humour, offer a riposte or a little flirtatious banter. She wishes she hadn't said it as the remark sits between them like a lead balloon. The swans are hoovering up the bread with their long black beaks.

'Actually, I'm quite creative,' he says suddenly and she smiles. But all she wants him to do is touch her as he begins to tell her how he built the boat, how he'd commissioned all the individual suppliers for each of the services, what a job it had been. She listens in silence wondering what it would be like to feel his skin against hers.

'Am I being boring?'

'Of course not,' she lies, trying to hide her disappointment. 'It's just I don't know anything about things like that.' Her mood dips. That hadn't been the right response. She feels wrong footed. Suddenly she misses Jack's dry humour, his ability to take the piss, to laugh at her seriousness because he wouldn't take her seriously at all.

The sun begins to sink into the horizon and the sky turns pink. Black and olive shadows form under the willows crosshatching the velvety water so it's hard to tell where the bank ends and the water begins.

'It's beautiful,' she says.

He goes to find his camera, but when he gets back the light has changed. He fiddles with the lens. 'How about just isolating the abstract shapes?' she suggests. 'It looks like a Mondrian,' she says thinking of the poster she'd bought with Jack at the Tate to hang over his bed. The inverted willows hang upside down reflected in the water as if part of a submerged city.

Like Venice, she thinks. Italo Calvino, she wants to add, but then decides not to.

'Classical or something else?' he asks, selecting a CD.

'I don't mind, you choose.'

'You're hard work,' he says putting on Van Morrison. She tries to dismiss the negative remark and wonders what prompted it. But once said it sinks into her mind like a stone.

The light is fading now as they take the dishes inside. She goes over and leans out of the window nearest the bank and her heart contracts at the sight of the black willows etched on the glassy water, the white swans drifting silently past like something out of a ballet. A great orange moon hangs low over the fields, almost at arm's length in a veil of mist; a solstice moon. Beside it there's a great gash in the clouds as if someone's taken a knife and tried to cut it out of the sky.

'Look at that,' she says. He comes up behind her and slips his arms round her waist. She shivers. They stand in the moonlight listening to the sounds of the river; the sudden splash of a water vole, a duck taking off or landing. He turns her towards him, lifts her T-shirt over her head and goes to undo her bra.

'Men can never do that.'

He lets it drop to the floor and runs his hands over her breasts, bending to take her nipples in his mouth and then removes the rest of her clothes so she's left stand-

ing naked in the window of the boat, dappled by moonlight, her skin silver as the scales of a fish.

'Do you mind if I roll a joint.'

She feels hurt. Isn't she enough?

'Whatever you like, it's your brain and your boat.'

'It just makes me feel even more tactile.'

'Come here and kiss me.'

She can taste the moon on his tongue. He kneels down
and she holds his head against her as if it was something
precious and cannot tell whether it is his mouth or the
rocking of the boat that is making her feel so light-
headed. This is what she needs; this is what she has always
needed. Suddenly she feels incredibly tender toward him.
He seems at home now in this place beyond ideas and
language, as he explores her body, it plains and valleys,
reaches inside her. He takes her to the bed. She runs her
fingers along his spine watching his unfamiliar face above
hers. His eyes are closed. He doesn't know she's watching.

After, she lays her head on his chest. She feels lost in
this new landscape. He is leaner than Jack, not as broad.
He smells different, like a city she's never visited before
where everything is unfamiliar.

'Where do you want to sleep?' he asks. 'Here or in the
spare bed? Alone? Together?'

'With you,' she says.

She goes to the tiny bathroom and cannot resist opening the cupboard as she pees. What's she looking for?
Clues? Signs? There are razors, a bottle of blue mouth
wash, and some expensive massage oil. Who, she

wonders, was the last recipient? When she gets back he's made up the bed with a white duvet and sheets. In the day it's a sofa.

4.00 a.m. and he's asleep beside her. She lies in the dark feeling the lull of the boat beneath, then climbs over him and goes to the window. The moon has moved, swung round almost to the other side of the boat. Shards of light craze the black water reflecting back a jigsaw moon. Mondrian's moon, she thinks.

What's she doing here? She always wants too much.

When she climbs back into bed beside him she curls her back towards him and places her foot on his leg to maintain contact but he is asleep and doesn't notice. Suddenly she feels very lonely. She should have tried harder to humour him earlier, not to have been so forth-right in her views on art and literature. She knows she offended him. Why had she done it? It had been a sort of test. She wants the meeting of minds as well as bodies.

She's too old for this.

She wonders about the other women who've slept here, what they'd been like? Younger, prettier? She wished, now, she'd brought some cream and cotton wool to take off her make up. She'd decided against it because it would have felt like a decision to stay the night before she even knew she was going to do so. But she'd put a tooth brush in her bag. So she'd been hedging her bets, then? She hopes she won't look too haggard in the morning.

He thinks she's younger than she is.

∾

She showers and dresses. For breakfast he offers her
coffee, eggs, strawberries and clotted cream in the galley
kitchen. She picks a few strawberries from the white bowl
and eats them off the stalks; she has to get back to London
and a meeting at the gallery. Suddenly it seems a long way
to go. She gathers up her things and he walks her back
up the duckboard path past the other boats and the smell
of frying bacon. The swans seem, somehow, less white in
the day light. She'll need a number to open the electronic
gate, he says, as he explains the route again: over two
roundabouts then across the bridge, after that take the
first left and she'll hit the road to the motorway. She can't
miss it. But she can. She should write it down, but doesn't
have a pen.

In the car park he kisses her goodbye.

'Thank you for coming. Don't get lost,' he says as she
climbs into the car, the space between them filled with
unasked questions.

∾

It's still hot. The air is heavy and the sky dark with the
threat of rain. She hopes she can get back before the
storm breaks. She manages to find the motorway without losing her way, even though she'd only half-listened to
his directions. But then at junction 3 there's a long tail-
back and she grinds to a standstill. Suddenly she wishes
she could do it all again. She hadn't managed it well. Why

had she let the thought of Jack intrude last night when they'd been sitting on the deck talking? Why does she still want him so much? She knows Jack won't be thinking about her, that she's already the past as far as he's concerned. Why did everything seem more desirable in retrospect?

The traffic is building as the warning lights slow everyone to 50 mph. Then as they grind to a halt in a big tail back she picks up her phone and texts Rod: 'Forgive me for being so complicated last night. You were a lovely host.' But that didn't sound quite right. The traffic is hardly moving. Her phone bleeps. 'I've been thinking, too. Not sure I'm ready to . . . .'

The text breaks off. The reception is bad on the motorway and she's only received half of it. But she knows the rest.

Her head is beginning to hurt from the stink of exhaust fumes bouncing from the hot tarmac through the open window. It feels strange to be in a car after the rhythm of the boat. At the next slip road she turns off and follows it for about a mile turning right into a country lane. It's a relief to be out of the traffic. She stops the car and gets out. In the field to her left is a herd of black and white cows like the plastic ones the children had for their wooden farmyard, which are now gathering dust somewhere in the loft for her future grandchildren. She locks the car door, crosses the road and climbs over the gate. Dry tussocks of grass poke through the cracked earth and scratch her legs through her linen trousers.

As she walks up the hill she hears a sound, a whinny-
ing, as a large bay stallion comes cantering down the slope
towards her. He stops a little way off, throws back his
head and snorts, stamping his front hoof against the hard
earth. His coat glistens in the afternoon heat and there's
a frill of white foam at the corners of his mouth. She
bends and picks a handful of tough grass and holds it out
to him. It's all she has. He trots up to her and nudges her
hand, nuzzling at the grass, which he pulls rather half-
heartedly as if to please her. He's probably 16 hands high,
a hunter, she assesses, remembering the years spent as a
small pigtailed girl mucking out ponies in the nearby
stables during her holidays. It had been horses then, not
art. Life had been simpler, her future as yet unwritten,
much of which she's now used up. As he chomps on the
tough clumps she can feel his hot breath on her palm,
the bristles on his fleshy pink nose. She pats his glistening
coat releasing a cloud of dust, and then leans her head
on the white blade between his eyes stroking his wiry
forelock, his pricked velvet ears. She can fee the muscles
in his neck rippling beneath her, the power of him, as
something breaks inside her.

∾

It is hot and the city feels chocked. It had taken her hours
to get home and now the storm that has been following
her is moving in from the west. Sitting in her room she
can still feel the lull of the river in her body, his skin on
her skin. Her hair smells of aftershave and horse. Outside

[75]

the sky is darkening and in the distance she can hear a rumble of thunder. Then there's a brief flash, and she counts how many miles away the storm is, before going to the window, pushing up the sash and gulping in the thick night air. Outside the moon is white and hard as bone. It has started to spit with rain and down the street she can hear a dog barking and someone is playing music: Van Morrison.

BERNINI AND LEOPARD SKIN

Simon Hoffman did not feel quite as sophisticated as he would, perhaps, have liked to feel standing in his socks—he was relieved he had put on new ones and not the ones with holes—as he waited in the queue at Stansted holding his brogues in his hand ready to place them in the X-ray machine. Now was probably not the best moment, as he removed the loose change from his trouser pockets, along with the belt that was holding up his lightweight kaki trousers, to put in the small plastic tray, to ask if this trip was really such a good idea. Kiera, he was aware, had been called over by one of the airport security staff who was opening her leopard skin vanity case and delving suspiciously into its depths. He wondered if hair tongs could be classed as a weapon and would, therefore, have to be left in the plastic box along with all the other nail scissors and pen knives that hadn't been allowed on board.

Hairbrushes, aerosols and deodorants, as well as several exotic looking pots and tubes of face cream, were spread out in front of her like the counter in some chaotic chemist's shop as the burly official advised her that either she would have to leave most of them behind or pack them in her luggage as they exceeded the legal liquid allowance permitted on board.

'Leave them behind? That's Christian Dior,' Kiera responded incensed. 'You must be joking.'

This was not a good start. Putting the Christian Dior in her luggage meant that Kiera had to pull back on her high suede boots, which she'd only just wriggled out of in order to place them in the X-ray machine, and go back out through security to the Check In. Simon could not help but feel a bit irritated. Surely she must have known. Everyone knew that there were liquid restrictions on flights. 'I'll meet you on the other side of passport control in the Costa Coffee lounge,' he said handing her her ticket.

Simon Hoffman was the senior editor of a firm that published glossy art books. Ostensibly he was on his way to the British School in Rome to do some research for a new illustrated edition on the Bernini sculptures. It was a place he had visited several times before and always enjoyed. The cordial social dinners at the long table with their mix of young artists and seasoned art historians in the fine Lutyens' building were always a pleasure. He liked being near the Villa Guilia, the country residence of Pope Julius III, with its splendid Etruscan collection and close enough to the centre of Rome to either walk in or catch a bus. It was his favourite city. Of course Venice and Florence were wonderful, but Rome always seemed, somehow, grittier, more real. For him it was the cradle of the arts, where antiquity, Christianity and modern humanism all coalesced. Certainly Rome had its tourists but they seemed quickly absorbed into its everyday life. He was not expected at the British School until the Monday evening and this was Friday morning. He had, in fact, been a little economical with Lucy about *la verité* concerning his travel arrangements. This had given him an extra weekend and it was this time that he was planning to spend with Kiera Hamilton. At 57, Simon was the most senior in the firm; admired rather than liked. He knew the right people but some found him a little self satisfied for he was the only one of the senior editors with a doctorate and that, he somehow felt, gave him the edge.

In Costa Coffee he ordered himself a double macchiato and waited for Kiera, trying not to mind that he was doing so, but feeling the annoyance somewhere in his bowels. He had known her now for about three months, if known was the right word. She had come to work in the office as a temp while his usual secretary, Dawn, was on maternity leave. She'd been sent from an agency they had not used before. When he had opened the door that morning he'd been taken aback by Kiera's long blonde hair and low cleavage and had thought, for a moment, that she must be in the wrong place, for she looked more like a star from Eurotrash than someone sent to help work on a book on Bernini. But despite her only embryonic interest in art she turned out to be more than proficient at indexing.

It had been the night that Lucy was out rehearsing Mozart's Requiem with the choir, (they had an important concert coming up at the Albert Hall), that Simon had casually suggested to Kiera that they might have a drink after work. They had gone to Kettner's in Soho, a favourite of his, and after the champagne one thing, as they say in Mills and Boon novels, had led to another. Over the next few weeks, whenever he could, Simon Hoffman would find his way to Kiera's rather dreary flat, which she shared at the bottom of Archway Road with another girl, who, apparently, was a nurse and never seemed to be there. He loved the lewd sex, the way she would keep on her black stockings and high heels while he fucked her and how, without any cajoling on his part, she would climb on top, pinning his hands above his head so that he couldn't move until he came. He simply could not get enough of her skin, silky and tanned from the sun bed, and her shaved muff or the fact that even in the middle of the month she would be so hot, that after an hour of strenuous fucking his stomach would be streaked with bright red blood.

He was not a conventionally handsome man, though he did like to think that he had a certain presence when he walked into a room. What looks he had once had whilst a young man at Oxford had somewhat faded; his hair had thinned and his girth expanded with Lucy's cooking. Lucy was a very good cook. In fact Lucy was exceptionally good at most things. A GP who specialised in family planning, she was also an excellent mother to his two teenage sons, Giles and Ben. Fluent herself in Italian, she possessed a beautiful singing voice and had recently taken up the harp, which she'd already mastered to a very high standard. Everyone constantly told him how very lucky he was to have such an intelligent and accomplished wife. Well, probably they were right. Yet somehow all this earnest achievement quietly got on his nerves and dulled his desire. He longed for a bit of spontaneous chaos. He knew that he should appreciate her attributes, but felt smothered by her efficiency, her achievements and tireless organisation. Did nothing ever get Lucy down? In all the years they had been together she was never anything other than resolutely cheerful. He wondered if there was a chink in her armour that he had not seen; but if there was it had, even after all this time, never been obvious to him. They rarely made love now, and when they did so he felt it a joyless duty, a question more of rubber and spermicides than sexual fulfilment. Yet he had the sneaking suspicion that the situation suited her and that after the boys were born she had been quite happy to let things drift. But he longed for something more, something that would make him feel— what? Renewed?

Looking at the boarding screens he was worried that Kiera wouldn't get back before the gate closed. He was beginning to get agitated when he saw her standing by the ladies chatting on her mobile. He waved trying not to feel annoyed and she waved back obviously intent on finishing her conversation. Then as they stood in the queue to board their flight her phone beeped twice. 'Who's that?' he asked, less casually than he'd intended, as she checked the text. 'Oh just a friend,' was her breezy response. The fact was that this was the first time that Simon had actually seen Kiera in a while. When they had first got together she seemed to enjoy the dinners in Soho or at that intimate little restaurant he knew hidden away in Highgate. But over the past six weeks or so he'd had no real idea what she had been up to. For every time he had tried to contact her he had got her voicemail and now that Dawn was back from maternity leave the secretarial agency had sent Kiera to work for a city hedge fund. Yet when the chance of this trip to Rome had come up he couldn't resist suggesting that she join him. The thought of her lithe body next to his for three nights was just too tempting. He had lain beside Lucy dreaming of kneeling behind Kiera's silky backside; though it was a nuisance that that particular position hurt his knee, damaged years before in a rugby match and which, as he had grown older, had continued to trouble him.

'Of course, it's all on me,' he said when he had finally got through. 'It's my little treat. We'll have a wonderful weekend. There's a lovely little hotel I know just off the Pincio garden, it looks over the Viale del Muro Torto above the Tiber. It's charming. You can watch the sun going down over Rome. We can easily get to the Villa Borghese to see the Berninis and I'll take you to the Pantheon. It's quite my favourite building in Rome. I know you will love it, Kiera.' Just as he was fastening his seat belt and about to switch off his mobile, Lucy texted to wish him a good trip.

'See you next week darling. Hope it all goes well. Enjoy yourself.'

On the flight Kiera insisted on a window seat, so that she could 'see', and also a bottle of champagne 'to get in the holiday mood', which was brought by a tall tanned steward in a crisp white shirt with blonde highlights. To Simon it was obvious that he was gay, but that didn't seem to stop Kiera from flirting outrageously.

What she really wanted to do, she said, well into her third glass of champagne, her hand resting intimately on Simon's arm, was buy some shoes and a bag. 'Rome's famous for its leather, Simon,' she confided, as if inform-ing him about the status of some obscure local painter or poet. 'And we ought to get you a nice jacket as well. Something a bit more casual. You need to treat yourself. You could look quite sexy, you know,' she said ruffling his hair like a child's, 'if you took a bit more trouble.'

This was going to be an expensive weekend.

∾

When they checked into the hotel he was disappointed to find that their room had twin beds. He was certain that he'd asked for a 'matrimonial suite'. He tried to point out the mistake in his rusty Italian to the porter, who was hovering for a tip, but it seemed there were no other vacant rooms and Simon did not relish making a fuss and appearing incompetent. The window looked down into a small cobbled courtyard full of bright red geraniums in terracotta pots and beyond was the fine public park laid out in the 19th century by Giuseppe Valadier, which was linked to the park of the Villa Borghese. It was a beautiful view and he could not help thinking how soon he would be able to stand at the window with Kiera after making love and watch the sun go down, an iced drink in one hand, the other resting on her naked bum. He went to the mini bar and poured them each a gin and tonic hoping that this would be the prelude to an hour or two of sex before dinner. But instead of joining him on the bed Kiera had stripped off and was already busy in the shower with the door locked behind her.

When she came out wrapped in fluffy white towels, she undid her turban and started to blow dry her hair, then dress in a lacy bra and rather tight sundress, before leaning in towards the big mirror to apply copious amounts of mascara. When this seemed to have been completed to her satisfaction, she pulled up her dress and wriggled into a pair of salmon pink thongs, smoothing the skirt back down over her hips. 'Come on, Simon, get ready,' she said turning her back to the mirror and checking her rear view. 'Let's hit the town. I want to find some strappy sandals; very high, very *la dolce vita* and a huge bag. Hurry up. But you'd better change that shirt; you can't possibly go out in that.'

By the time they got to dinner, he was exhausted. They had been to six shoe shops and she must have tried on at least twenty pairs. In the end she'd chosen some highly impractical golden stilettos and a pair of scarlet wedge sandals. It had already cost him €300 and they had been in Rome less than five hours. As they ate their *gnocchi alla*

Romana and the *saltimbocca* that he always ordered at this particular restaurant, her phone beeped continually. Why did he not say anything, he wondered, as he ordered another bottle of Valpolicella, feeling his mood darken? But he refused to appear put out.

The single beds proved to be a bit of a problem, they couldn't, it turned out, be easily pushed together for there was a low tessellated table between them which was too heavy to move. After what, though he didn't like to admit, seemed like some rather desultory and obligatory (on her part) love making, Kiera complained in the early hours that she was too hot and that Simon was taking up all the room in her narrow bed, even though he knew that a good third of him was hanging over the edge. So reluctantly he climbed out, crossing the strait of polished marble floor, to spend the rest of the night in the twin. Drowsily drunk, he fell into a deep sleep, dimly aware that much of the night he was snoring.

∾

When he woke, the sun was streaming through the shutters and he could hear voices and a motor bike revving in the narrow street. His head hurt. He knew he shouldn't have ordered that other bottle of wine. As he turned over, tangled in the sweaty sheet, it took him a moment to realise that Kiera was not in her bed. The only evidence that she had ever inhabited it was a pair of dirty lace kickers caught in the covers. He got up and looked in the bathroom where the entire contents of her leopard skin vanity case — tampons, eye shadow and face bronzer — seemed to have been strewn round the big white sink. Naked, he sat down on the satin chair in the bedroom by the mini bar and picked up his phone. She had sent him a text. '*Ciao!* Gone to the Via del Corso to look for a bag. Boy at desk told me best shops there. C u later, babe.' He showered and shaved wondering whether he should text her back and if so what he should say. He had been planning, this morning, to take her to the Pantheon. He never failed to be moved by this ancient temple that had been built by Agrippa and re-built by Adrian before being turned into a church in the 7th century. He loved the majesty of its great dome, the diameter of which was equal to its height and which, for him, was one of the wonders of the world. How could she have preferred to go shopping rather than see that for the first time?

After he dressed, he wandered in its general direction, stopping to have an espresso in a little side street by the Santa Maria sopra Minerva. Rome was already going about its business and the narrow streets were bright with May sunshine as housewives in spotless blouses and coiffed hair went to buy bread and macaroni. In the barber's opposite, clients sat wrapped in large white gowns having their hair (and ears) trimmed or waiting, their faces covered with foam, to be shaved. He texted her: 'I'm having a coffee. I'll wait for you here,' giving her the name of the street while ordering another espresso as he watched the fishmonger over the road cleaning the scales off a bucket of pink and silver fish. Foolishly, he had not bought a book and kept looking at the creeping hand of his watch before, in a mounting state of frustration, getting up and making his way to the Doria Pamphilli. He had been sitting waiting under the stripped awning for over an hour as the shop keepers had scrubbed their steps and the owner of the hardware store, his huge stomach held up by a big leather belt, had smoked a cigarette and still there was no sign of Kiera.

He would go and see the Caravaggio. He would not waste any more time. Yet as he arrived at the entrance in the Piazza del Colligio Romano he saw, to his annoyance, that the museum attendant was already putting up the closed sign. He looked at his watch. It was ten past one and the gallery shut at one. He had wasted the whole morning. Standing on the steps he put his hand in his jacket pocket to search for his phone and noticed that there was a voice message, which he assumed must be from Kiera. He had not heard it ring and realised that when he had gone briefly into Santa Maria to look at the Filippino Lippi's he had turned it onto silent. When he pressed play he was surprised to hear Lucy. 'Simon, I've been trying to get you for the last few hours and had nothing but your voicemail. Please phone me, *immediately*. It's really urgent.'

He was taken aback by her insistence. It was not like Lucy at all to sound so agitated. Could she have somehow found out about Kiera? If so how? If she had he knew he would have to concoct some story, though at that moment he couldn't quite imagine what. For Lucy the basis of their nearly twenty years of marriage had been trust and loyalty. Surely, someone who made a virtue of these qualities would not have stooped to reading his emails? He stood on the steps of the Doria Pamphilli unsure what to do next; and he was not a man used to feeling unsure. Still there was no message from Kiera, but he would not, he decided, demean himself by ringing her. What on earth could Lucy possibly want, he thought irritably. Surely it couldn't be that important. He would ring her later when he'd had time to think of a suitable response. He might as well make what he could of the rest of the day and decided to head back to the hotel by way of the Spanish Steps and visit the Bernini Fountain of the Barcaccia that stood near the house where John Keats had died.

Back at the hotel he found a corner table in the small glass covered restaurant and ordered a large campari and soda and a plate of *antipasti*. The restaurant was crowded and at the large central table a group was obviously celebrating a birthday. A woman of a certain age with an extravagant bouffant of red hair, immaculate makeup and a clutch of gold bangles on her tanned and wrinkled arm seemed to be the guest of honour. Italians, he decided, certainly knew how to celebrate. Knocking back the campari, he then ordered a bottle of Gringolino to go with his roasted baby artichokes, salami and mortadella. He was still a little hung-over from the night before, despite this morning's coffees. But he no longer cared. As the alcohol started to hit his blood stream he began to calm down after the morning's frustrations and humiliations. Aware that it was working its way down into his groin, he shifted on the hot leather seat to loosen his tightening trousers, though there seemed little chance now that there would be a siesta with Kiera this afternoon. Still, the day after tomorrow he would check into the British School. That was what he had come for. There he would get back to work and be among people who would appreciate what he was doing. Just as he was about to tuck into his fegato alla venezia, his phone rang again. He almost wished, now he was beginning to enjoy his lunch that Kiera wouldn't bother.

'Simon? Simon? Is that you? Thank God. Didn't you get my message to phone? I've been trying to get you all morning. Why didn't you ring me back? ' Lucy's voice was frantic.

'Sorry, darling,' he answered as nonchalantly as he could. 'Been in the library. Had the phone off. What's up that's so important and can't keep?'

'Simon, it's Giles. He's had an accident.'

'What? What do you mean? What sort of accident?'

'I got a call from the school this morning just after I got into work. He was knocked off his bike in the Holloway Road. A lorry the police said. I'm not sure. We're in UCH. He has just been down in the X-ray department. They've been doing a scan. They found him lying in the road unconscious and brought him into A&E. Oh God, Simon, he's all bruised and broken. He looks so young, so vulnerable, just like he did when he was ten,' and he can hear that she is no longer able to hold back her sobs. 'Simon, I'm frightened. Please, please come home.'

When she rang off, he sat in the middle of the restaurant with the *fegato alla venezia* growing cold in front of him, unable to move or gather his scattered thoughts. It felt as if his heart had stopped; no, more accurately, as if someone had pulled it out like a plug from a socket. What the hell was he doing here playing lothario when his son was lying in intensive care, drainage tubes up his broken nose, his arm hooked up to a monitor? He stood up quickly and pushed back his chair, throwing down the white damask napkin onto his unfinished meal, and dashed to the lift. In the bathroom he grabbed his wash bag and shaving things from among the debris of Kiera's makeup and threw them into his bag. Would he get a seat on the plane? Surely at this time of day there would be something.

How could he have been such a bloody fool? Poor Lucy must have been frantic trying to call him, having to go to the hospital all on her own. He imagined her trying to find a parking place, running up to the ward to find her son unconscious and dressed in an unfamiliar hospital gown. Would he be too late? For a split second he wondered whether this was some sort of divine retribution. Oh God, please let him be alright. And suddenly it all came rushing back, the Sunday mornings teaching the boys to swim at the Caledonian leisure centre, the summer holidays in Salcombe building dams and moats on the beach, the Christmases when they had been small spent with Lucy's parents at the farm in Sussex.

His family, his life. How careless he had been of them.

If he had been anyone else he would have told him that he was being a jerk for cheating on his dedicated accomplished wife with a girl that he now admitted to himself looked like a second rate porn star. He was a cultured man. What had he thought he was doing? It was such a cliché, like something from a cheap TV sitcom, and he had succumbed to it. Been tempted and flattered by the fake tan and over-exposed flesh. Why had he let his dick rule his head? What had he wanted? To prove he was immortal, that age was not slowly eating him away at the edges? That he was somehow immune? And now his son, his dear son with his crooked smile and a passion for Arsenal, was in intensive care. Why hadn't he spent more time with him instead of bawling him out for leaving his wet towels on the bathroom floor and for the loud music pounding from his bedroom?

At the check-out desk he hardly knew what he was doing as he asked for the bill and a cab to the airport. It would, the porter told him, be ten minutes. Unable to keep still he paced nervously backwards and forwards across the marble lobby in front of the fountain that trickled into a pool of carp when he looked up and saw, through the glass extension that lead to the bar, Kiera sitting propped on a bar stool flirting with the barman. She was wearing a very short white skirt and the new red wedge sandals that he had bought her yesterday. In one hand she was holding a cocktail while the other was placed conspiratorially on the barman's arm as she leant forward whispering something into his ear that made them both laugh. Simon stood transfixed, unable to feel anything, as if watching a film.

When the porter called to indicate that the taxi had arrived he picked up his bag, ran out and jumped in slamming the cab door behind him, desperately hoping that the Roman traffic would not be too heavy. How long would it take, he wondered, before Kiera noticed that he'd gone? Still that was no longer his problem. The only thing that mattered now was making it to the airport and getting a seat on the plane. He texted Lucy to tell her he was on his way. Suddenly, more than anything else, he wanted to be at home, wanted to be with his wife, holding her hand and wishing their son well.

Nothing else mattered.

What an idiot he had been. God, Giles must be alright and if he was, he would never, ever stray again. He knew that this was a cheap plea bargain but it was all he had. At the airport he rushed across what seemed like acres of marble to the Alitalia desk. There was a flight leaving in fifteen minutes. They would let him board as an emergency in the circumstances. He hardly knew what he was doing or which way he was going as he ran along what seemed the endless miles of corridor to the gate arriving just before it closed. As he put his bag in the overhead compartment and took his seat he could feel his wet shirt sticking to his back and his hands shaking. When he looked up, as the steward in the yellow inflated life jacket was going through the safety instructions, he noticed that he was same one with blonde highlights who, on the flight over, had served them champagne. Passengers, he was reminding them, must turn off all electrical equipment for the take off. As Simon reached for his phone to turn it to flight mode he quickly texted Lucy.

'Will be with you soon. Hang on. Will all be alright. Love you.'

He was such a lucky man. Please God that he had not realised it too late. Giles would be alright. He had to be alright. His little family would survive. He would book a cottage in Salcombe after this and take a week off. They would all go together like they used to when the boys had been small and Giles could take it easy and convalesce, he would read to him like he had when he had been small. He would make it up to Lucy. When he landed he would phone the British School to let them know that he wouldn't be coming; that he'd been called home urgently on a family matter and that the book on Bernini would just have to wait.

GOYA'S DARK

The light is fading as the evening draws in across the banana plantation. It laps round the walls of the Marimanti Rural Methodist Centre where she is the only guest like the incoming tide. Down the long hallway she can hear the tinny amplification of the TV at full volume where the caretaker is taking advantage of the single hour of electricity, provided by the ineffectual generator, before they are plunged into complete darkness. He is sitting in his vest, his dark skin covered with beads of sweat; his dusty feet up on a white plastic chair in the middle of the large room that is used for Bible conferences. Swatting flies and swigging beer from the neck of a bottle he scratches his groin as he watches the election rally, which flickers in the corner on the black and white set that's normally covered by a lace nylon cloth.

She doesn't much like him. There is something insolent and over familiar about his manner; quite different to all the other Kenyans she has met. The other evening he had walked into her room without knocking as she was standing wrapped in nothing but a towel, to tell her to stop using her hairdryer.

'Makes TV picture go,' he had said without apology.

The sound of the set bounces off the lino floors and metal window frames, echoing through the empty rooms of the long concrete bungalow that's the only substantial building for miles amid the scattering of wooden shacks and mud huts with their corrugated tin roofs. She can hear the voice of the opposition leader Raila Odinga haranguing President Mwai Kibaki. There are still months to go before the election, but her heart sinks every time she hears the obvious barefaced lies about bringing electricity, roads and secondary education to all the people of Kenya. For ever since she has been here she's watched the women trudging in the heat backwards and forwards from the river with oil drums of untreated water strapped to their backs and the barefoot children in patched uniforms trailing the five miles to school in the early morning along unmade roads.

She looks out of the window and sees a young boy in a torn T-shirt, grubby shorts and battered flip flops making his way home in the fading light over the dusty fields with a bundle of firewood. The fields are cracked and dry as the soles of his feet and he is caked in red dust.

She gets up and gathers her torch, her mobile phone and glasses and places them under the mosquito net next to her pillow. Her room is clean but spare. There is a desk, on which there is a copy of the Gideon Bible in fake green leather, and two beds covered in incongruous pale blue flowered satin bedspreads ruched with pink nylon, the sort of cheap decorations that she images you might find in a brothel. Hanging above each is a blue mosquito net. She searches for some matches and melts the stub of a thin candle onto a chipped saucer so that she will be prepared when the lights suddenly go out. That has been the hardest part, the dark. When she'd arrived here in the charity land rover from Nairobi all she had been able to see was a huddle of shacks and groups of shadowy figures lit by the occasional paraffin lantern.

As they had driven north from Nairobi to Embu the soil had been bright red and the landscape lush with banana crops. Del Monte, the canned fruit company, grew pineapples in the region and because it was October the purple jacaranda trees were in bloom. On their way up country they had passed through Central Province with its emerald tea plantations and green paddy fields, its small towns —villages, really—where women sat selling fists of bananas or ripe avocados under the shade of torn rice sacks. Then the tarmac had given way to rutted dirt roads and scrub with Biblical scenes of herdsmen and women with sticks poking wayward goats and skinny hump-backed cattle, or caravans of camels driven down from Ethiopia to be slaughtered for meat. She had seen decrepit, moth-eaten donkeys, pulling heavy carts loaded with wood or sacks of maize, being beaten with vicious leather whips by their drivers. She was no animal-rights activist, but it had been hard to watch.

As they had driven over the dust roads she had noticed how formally everyone was dressed despite the sweltering heat; the men in pleat-fronted trousers and long-sleeved shirts, the women in skirts, blouses and neat jackets, as if going to work in a building society. Poverty, it seemed, made people want to appear respectable. And everywhere there had been churches. Some of brick with garish stained glass windows built by the Anglicans, the Catholics, the Methodists or the Seventh Day Adventists, others simply rundown shacks that announced themselves as the 'Word of God Tabernacle' or the 'Apostolic Pentecostal Church'. Religion was, she'd been told by the other aid workers, big business and many a self-appointed pastor had gone from being a goat herder to wearing a pink designer suit and owning a big shiny car on the tithes paid by his flock. Sunday mornings in Marimanti were a crackle of amplified singing and preaching.

As they had driven on, the light had begun to fade so that by the time they had crossed the final dry river bed into the township she'd felt as if she had been transported back several centuries. In truth, she had been a little afraid. What was she doing alone here amid the arid scrub of this remote region of Kenya's Eastern Province, a woman of sixty, more at home taking a Sunday stroll across Hampstead Heath with her cocker spaniel than sitting in a Land Rover beside an unknown African driver?

Divorce, it seems, had unforeseen consequences, especially late in life.

When Richard had asked her in a contrite moment, while packing his books to take to Chloe's, what she would do now, she had simply replied, 'I don't know; survive somehow.' Still she had not quite expected this.

Though she had been told when she had decided to come out here and teach that there would be no infrastructure, no roads, no running water or electricity, it was still a shock. Beyond the car's headlights there had been nothing but the deep blackness of the huge African night broken only by hundreds of stars embroidering the tent of inky sky. The dark had had an unfamiliar density. It seemed impenetrable.

Looking at the silhouettes huddled outside the shacks ringed by halos of lamplight from the hanging storm lanterns, she had thought, for some reason, of Goya's Black Paintings. There was something about the dark that had the same intensity as those strange works that Goya, at the age of 72, deaf and nearing the end of his difficult life, had reputedly painted onto the walls of the *Quinta del sordo*—the house of the deaf man, as his rustic farm house had become known. Embittered by the turbulence of the Napoleonic Wars, he had moved there with his 20 year old companion, Leocadia Weiss, and begun to paint directly onto the plaster of the upper floors some of the most disturbing images of darkness ever painted. The Black Paintings had neither been commissioned nor were they ever sold and during Goya's lifetime no one ever reported seeing them. What dark demons had he been describing, she wonders, what psychological depths he had been plumbing?

The death of reason or the end of hope? It was hard to tell.

Although she had now been here for several weeks, she had still not got used to the dark and the long nights

when, hot and unable to sleep, she would lie waiting for
the pale haze of dawn and the cock's first crow. That's
why she had gathered everything under the mosquito net;
her torch, her glasses, and mobile phone for once the
lights went out she would not be able to find anything.
She had tried reading by torch light, remembering doing
so as a child under the blanket when she had been in love
with Jo in *Little Women* for having the courage to cut off her
long hair. But reading in such bad light hurt her eyes and
she could not get comfortable. At nine on the dot the
lights go out. The silence is almost as intense as the dark.
She goes to the window and stares into the huge African
night that seems to spread on and on into the infinity of
the bush. Then she draws the curtains tight, weighing
down the corners with the Gideon Bible and her Kenyan
guide book to keep out the mosquitoes and the host of
flying insects that nightly invade her room.

It is too early to sleep, but there is nothing else to do.
She is too hot and her hair sticks to her forehead and neck
as she tosses and turns under the mosquito net so that she
feels like a newly netted fish, for it is too small for the
bed and keeps falling onto her face making her feel quite
claustrophobic. She wants to throw it off, but knows there
is malaria in the area. Finally she falls into a fitful sleep
to be woken by something flitting across her face. She
sits up in a panic, her heart pounding, and feels for her
torch to find a large green beetle rattling around inside
the net. She flaps it open and clambers out, hearing the
beetle fall with a thud to the lino. She wonders if it might
be some sort of scorpion. As she reaches for her torch to

look more closely the ray of light makes it skitter across the floor. She goes to the desk and picks up the plastic water jug, takes off the blue lid and places the jug upside down trapping the thing. Now it is safely inside the jug she shines the torch on it, watching it trying to climb the slippery opaque sides, fascinated and disgusted by its hinged black legs. Back in bed she tucks the mosquito net tightly around her and attempts to sleep but feels choked by the dark, like someone being slowly suffocated by a length of velvet.

Once before all this she had been someone and the someone she had been then would never have come here. And now she was, who? She doesn't know. Thirty years as Richard's wife, when they had been described as one of the most solid marriages in television had not left her prepared for these solitary nights in the African bush. She and Richard had met at Cambridge. He had written for the Footlights. She had acted. It had been a grand passion though it had been a few years before they had finally got together. But men aged better than women. He was in the public eye, while she'd given up the theatre to publish children's books and have two children of her own. She had grown middle-aged. He had grown distinguished. It was a cliché but he'd left her for his production assistant who was more than twenty years younger. But clichés are only clichés because they are so often true. And now Chloe was pregnant.

She had joked with her friends about running away to Africa. And then had decided why not? It was the sort of thing people always talked about and never did. She did not want to be one of those sorts of people. Unlike Doctor Johnson, she had grown tired of London. It no longer made sense. She had taken early retirement. Not because she wanted to, but because it was made clear by the publishers for whom she had worked for more than twenty years that they now wanted a younger team. The sorts of children's books she enjoyed publishing were not the ones they considered commercial. Too wordy, too old fashioned. The sort she had loved reading to Sam and Poppy when they had been small.

Her children? Well that was another reason why she was here. They wouldn't admit it, she was sure, but they seemed embarrassed by her. Now they had grown up and left home she felt redundant, an inconvenience. They had their own partners, their own lives that did not include her. When she rang to see them they were always busy; she felt like a burden, a duty she was asking them to perform. It was easy for them to see Richard, to have dinner in Shoreditch in a fashionable bar or at Soho House with him and Chloe who was nearly their contemporary, but they knew she needed their company, not to feel alone and bereft, not to feel as though her life had been pointless and without meaning. It had been so much easier when she had been married to their father. Then they had not had to think about her except if they needed her or on regulation holidays such as Christmas. But a single woman of sixty is an inconvenience, even to her children.

So she had decided to come to Africa. She had simply rung the charity she'd supported for a number of years and suggested it. It hadn't been hard. She was more than qualified. After an armful of injections here she was listening to the great African night wash up against her window. Lying in the dark she wondered why she had really come. Of course there was the reason she had given to friends about doing something altruistic because they, in the west, all had so much. 'Well I think you're really brave,' Val had said over a valedictory bottle of Merlot at her kitchen table in Muswell Hill. 'I know I couldn't do it.' But she'd known in her heart of hearts that had not really been the point.

Wasn't it a test of sorts to find out who she was, now she was no longer needed as a wife, a mother or a publisher, now she was surplus to requirements? Sam had even phoned to say that he had told his father about the trip. 'Actually Mum, Dad's rather impressed.' Impressed? She had paid a high price for her thirty years of motherhood and apparently stable marriage. There was a point, say ten or fifteen years ago, when she'd still felt comparatively young, still in the thick of things, when she and Richard had talked about how they would spend these years, how they would buy an old farm house in the Limousin, which was so much cheaper and less spoilt than the Dordogne, and do it up, stripping it back to the original beams and revealing old fireplaces, so they could spend summers there drinking the local wine on the terrace when their friends and when the children came to stay. It had never occurred to her that life, as those great philosophers the Beatles had once said, was what happened when you were busy making other plans.

She needs to pee and reaches for the torch. As she makes her way barefoot to the tiny bathroom with its one tap and lavatory without a seat, she can't resist shining the light onto the upturned water jug to check on the beetle. To her horror it's not there. She has no idea how it escaped and shines her torch into the deep dark corners of the room and sees that it has scuttled under the bed. What brute strength had enabled it to shift the jug? Nervously she picks up a sheet of paper, sliding it underneath the hard green carapace and plopping the jug down quickly before it can escape again. Then she reaches for the Gideon Bible, which she places on top of the jug to weigh it down.

Perhaps it will respond to the word of God.

When she gets back into bed she can't sleep. Apart from the caretaker snoring on his mattress at the other end of the concrete building she must be the only person for miles around. The Mission Centre is outside the small township and there is nothing else under the wide night sky except the banana plot surrounded by endless scrub. She wonders what would happen if she was suddenly taken ill, what she would do in the middle of all this dark and feels a mounting sense of isolation and panic. If she died, would Richard mind? Would her children? Or would their lives simply go on, her presence washed away like a footprint in the sand? On the flight over she had realised how arbitrary death really was. For somewhere above Ethiopia they had hit terrible turbulence and the captain had asked the crew to return to their seats and for everyone to fasten their seat belts. For nearly an hour the plane had rattled and bumped through the clouds as if white water rafting. She had been convinced that it could not withstand such pressure and had hid her head under the blanket certain that she was about to die. Though she had not, she might well have.

That was the point. Death was always so much closer than one realised. And now at 60, how many more years did she have left? And if neither Poppy nor Sam had children, say, for ten years, how long would she know her grandchildren? As to great grandchildren, well she would probably never see them. Three generations, that is all it takes for us to disappear from living memory. We are just a blip, she thinks, as she remembers her own grandmother, how she had loved to go and stay with her in Southwold and sit on the brick step behind the kitchen in her lovely little garden smelling of tobacco plants and antirrhinum, shelling broad beans or making perfume in a milk bottle from pink rose petals which she'd shredded and covered with olive oil. But now she feels like Goya must have felt; that the dark was triggering her deepest fears which the daylight kept veiled.

She tries to think of times when she'd felt more positive about the dark and remembers when the children had been little and they'd spent Christmas with Richard's parents in the Mendips. They had always attended the village carol service, walking to the small 15th century church across the green and up the yew-lined path wrapped in scarves and thick winter coats, following Richard's father who always led the way, shepherding his little flock with a large torch. The children had gathered round the crib holding candles to light the cold dim church that had been decorated with ivy and holy. She was not even a believer, but there had been something about the flickering candle light, the children's clear voices reaching to the vaulted rafters and the dark Somerset countryside enclosing the old stone church, which had remained the same for centuries that touched her to the core. Then they had gone home and had warm mince pies and sherry by a blazing log fire while the children had laid out their stockings and written their Christmas letters. It had been a measure of something precious, something that could not quite be grasped, something that had made her want to cry because she knew that such moments were only fleeting, that even as she was experiencing them they were already slipping away; that her children would grow up and leave, that the age of innocence would end.

Is that what Goya had painted? The end of innocence, the death of a future? Is that what his ghastly Saturn eating one of his own children meant? She thinks of those nightmarish paintings where the faces seem to dissolve and the people have no eyes or mouths and appear to gaze blankly at nothing, their silent cries echoing out in the arid landscape. It is a world where there is no comfort, no redemption from the dark, where there is no escape from life's failures and where even children holding candles in the holy hush of an English church on a cold December night are not enough to keep the fear of loneliness, death and unreason at bay.

And yet wasn't Africa supposed to be her redemption? Hadn't she come here to reclaim some sense of purpose in her collapsed life? She tries not to think of Richard in Chloe's flat, the new baby due only a couple of months away now, tries not to torture herself imagining his familiar body, known for so many years from its muscular firmness to its middle aged fullness, curled naked and warm around his new young fecund wife as once he had wrapped his arms around her feeling for Poppy dancing in her stretched stomach. She runs her hands across her breasts and down her thighs. It is a long time since she has been touched, but still she remembers as if it was yesterday that intimacy of skin on skin and wonders if her fingers will ever smell of sex again.

How did she get to be this old, how had it happened? This is not what she had meant at all; no, this is not what she had intended. And love? What had happened to love?

The silence seems to become more and more intense as if she is losing her sense of hearing as well as sight. Suddenly she thinks of Marlow sitting stranded on the Thames in the fog waiting to leave for the Congo, how he'd described a queer feeling coming over him, a feeling of being an impostor and that instead of travelling to the centre of a continent, he'd felt as if, in some way, he was about to set off for the centre of the earth. Perhaps that's what she feels too, as if she is an impostor, that she's only been masquerading as a wife and a mother and has now been revealed in her true colours. Peace, Marlow had said, that was what he was after. Was that why she was here, to ward off that larger dark and find peace? Like Goya,

Marlow's voyage had been a personal quest, an attempt to discover who he was, to find out whether there were any moral absolutes in this Godless world. Is that what she's looking for after thirty years of marriage? Moral certainty? An essential self?

And if she was to find it, what then?

Being here has been difficult. Not just at night, but also during the day. She's hated the boredom of having nothing to do when she's not teaching, for there's nowhere to go outside the charity compound as the town consists of no more than a few shacks selling plastic buckets, bottles of water, batteries and cheap flip-flops or hands of bruised bananas and bags of rice. The day is punctuated by her classes and the meals taken with the other aid workers in the straw lean-to at the back of the kitchen where Moses, wrapped in his big white apron, waves to her from the kitchen door as she toys with a plate of stringy goat curry mopped up with bland white maze bread or a dish of 'green grams', which give her terrible indigestion. But at least when it's light her mind is taken up with teaching or ways of keeping cool and she doesn't have to face the great silence that the night throws up, which though not filled, as for Marlow, with the tremor of far-off drums, is with something equally fearful, yearning and lonely.

She wonders what time it is and looks at the illuminated face of her mobile phone. Only three o'clock and another four hours to go before it will be light. She can hear the cry of some small animal in the scrub and wonders whether Chloe and Richard will have a boy or a girl and what it will be called and whether Sam and Poppy will take to having a half-brother or sister young enough to be their own. How strange that a new child will be born to the man with whom she has spent most of her life and yet it will be utterly separate and apart from her, grow up without any reference to her. She feels more and more pushed to the outside of what had once been her family. Finally, just before dawn, she slips into an exhausted sleep.

She is woken by the light creeping in under the anchored curtains. She stretches, her limbs aching from the hard bed and lumpy pillow, aware that she has had a fretful night, but uncertain in the harsh beam of morning sun now shining through the window what had so frightened her. As she climbs out of bed to wash her face and comb her damp hair she can't resist checking to see if the beetle is still inside the plastic jug. It is sitting there motionless under the Gideon Bible. She wonders if it is dead, if it has suffocated. Do beetles need to breathe? She is not sure.

She goes and splashes cold water over her face and ties back her hair washing beneath her armpits and breasts with the cold water from the single tap. This morning she is teaching Class Six again. She is coming to the end of her final week now. On her first day they had stood up when she'd entered the dirt floored class room and welcomed her in formal unison. Some of the children were barefoot but all wore strangely old fashioned uniforms, though often they were ragged and patched; long shorts for the boys and tunics with blouses for the girls, as if they'd just tumbled out of the Beano. They had been shy and hidden their faces and bad teeth coyly behind their hands when she'd first spoken to them or asked them for answers. When they were sitting down it was sometimes hard to tell which were the boys and which the girls for they all had the same shorn heads. She had got them writing stories and even rudimentary poems, had worked on similes and metaphors. They had been respectful and well behaved. A little passive and unused to thinking for themselves, perhaps, but she had enjoyed watching them grow in confidence and begin to bloom. Regularly, when she came back into the classroom, after taking a mug of hot sweet tea with the other teachers, boiled up with milk and sugar in a large kettle in the earthen floored staff room, she'd find a fat white hen sitting under one of the desks.

And now she will be leaving in three days and going back to whatever London has to throw at her. She doubts if she'll ever come back, ever see these people again. These weeks have been like living in a parallel world. Slowly she has got to know a little about these children's lives. How Mercy has to get breakfast everyday before school for her four brothers and sisters and how, although no one admits it, Gloria dropped out of class because one night she had, though only twelve, been secretly circumcised ready for an older man, a practice still tacitly sanctioned by some of the women as a means of reducing sexual appetite, and how Joseph is often absent because his mother is sick, and his father has left, and he has to plough the family plot in order to feed his younger brothers and sisters.

Hot and covered in dust she sits in a corner of the classroom sipping her bottle of warm water during the afternoon break, trying to summon the energy to teach the last lesson, when a group of girls from Class Six gathers around her. Shyly they ask why she came to Kenya, if she is married, if she has any children and what their names are and what has happened to her husband. Is she old or young, they ask giggling, and will she ever come back to see them? And suddenly she can feel their hands running through her dusty foreign hair and touching her skin as if they still can't quite believe it. And as she laughs, holding out her white arm next to their ebony ones feigning surprise, they turn away burying their heads shyly on each others shoulders, covering the wide smiles which have broken out across their open black faces.

OI YOI YOI

'**H**ello, darling', he says distractedly, as she bends to kiss him. The endearment is somehow generic, reserved for anyone to whom he might be close, even the dog. His skin is dry against her cheek, and blotched with liver spots.

'Hello, daddy', she answers, hoping that this will give him a clue and remind him that she is neither his dead wife nor her own daughter. He is sitting in a chair by the window in a beam of pale spring sun staring out onto the bed of savagely pruned rose bushes poking through their mulch of fresh manure. She places the bunch of narcissi she has bought in the small water jug and thinks of the garden of the house where she grew up; the herbaceous borders with their poppies and blue lupins, the conservatory with its pots of cacti and smell of wet earth where he used to sit on Sunday mornings to read the papers. Outside her mother would be deadheading the roses, a turtle dove purring in the distant beeches.

But the garden he is looking at now is unimaginative and utilitarian. There are a couple of benches set on the gravel with brass plaques screwed to the backs, presumably dedicated by grateful family members of past residents. When it is warm enough she imagines that the guests, as they are called, sit out there with their cups of tea and digestive biscuits. On the wall, near the car park, a thrush is breaking open a snail with its beak.

Her father is dressed in a checked viyella shirt, brown corduroy trousers and a cashmere jumper, his weekend clothes; though now this is what he wears every day and they are rather worn. Years ago, during the week, he wore beautifully cut, pin striped suits and a silk tie. He was always a dapper man. In those days he ran a gallery in Cork Street specialising in British Modern Art. Ben Nicholson, Naum Gabo, Patrick Heron. That sort of thing. First and second generation artists from St. Ives. The only indication that this is what he once did is a framed poster, hung over the bed, of Roger Hilton's *Oi Yoi Yoi*, with its flat patches of orange and blue, and the loose black outline of a woman with large bouncing breasts.

Her father had always liked attractive women. Hilton had told him, one day when her father was visiting his studio, that it was of his wife dancing on the verandah, that they had been having a quarrel. She was nude and angry and jumping up and down shouting 'oi yoi yoi'. Her father liked to tell that story. He liked the fact that he knew the artists he sold. She can't image what the other residents make of it. Too outré, too odd. It seems incongruously affirmative here, in the circumstances; too full of life.

A remembrance of things past.

His ivory hairbrushes and shaving things, a small radio and some pots of pills are arranged neatly beside a clutch of photographs on the top of the chest of drawers. There is her mother in a flowered dress sitting in the hammock with the dog at her feet, a graduation photograph of her brother, Toby, his unruly hair cascading from under his mortar board in that summer of '68, and one of her as a schoolgirl standing by a laurel hedge in a checked summer dress. She can't remember when it was taken. These few things and the poster are all that distinguish this room from all the others down the hall.

As she kisses her father his smell takes her back to being a child, and those mornings when she and Toby were eating their boiled eggs before school, and he would come down stairs and thrust out his newly shaved cheek for them to kiss. It was always the same, that slight tilt and turn of his fragrant face, which he simply presented to them. He never kissed them first. The pomade he wore came from Penhaligons in Piccadilly. A bottle still stands on the dressing table, the tangy scent of citrus overlaying the other smells in the room — the Pledge air freshener, the cooking that seeps in from down the corridor and something harder to define, something yeasty and fermenting, the odour of decay.

'Where are my glasses?' her father asks of no one in particular, looking round distractedly for the battered leather case, though why he should want them she is not sure, for his eyesight, since her mother died, is now so bad that he can no longer read. 'Here they are, daddy,' she says, gently placing them in his hands and closing his bony fingers around the familiar case, but he turns away as if he has already forgotten what he asked for.

It feels odd that she still addresses him by the same name she used as a child — daddy. There is something awkward about the word coming out of the mouth of a middle aged woman, for it presupposes a relationship they do not really have. Yes, she is his daughter, and he is her father, but there are so many lost years and now she is not even sure he knows who she is. But she is here because of those filial ties. She is testing the thickness of blood.

But maybe that's the point. Maybe she is no more a stranger to him now than she was when she was young. He wasn't exactly a hands on father. She doesn't have a single memory of him playing with her as child. No recollection of cricket on the beach or of him helping her build sandcastles or teaching her to swim; no memory of him ever reading her stories or hearing her tables, which, she realises, she still doesn't know. It was her dutiful mother who came to parents' evenings, who took them to the dentist and the pantomime at Christmas. He may have gone to watch Toby play cricket for his school once, but she can't remember him ever having shown any real interest in anything she did. Though there was that time, for some reason that she now can't remember, that they had driven to the sea. Somewhere in Sussex, near Rye. She can still recall the cloying smell of the Humber's leather seats that hot July afternoon and the drone of the engine as the tarmac seemed to melt under the wheels, while Toby kept asking if they were nearly there. They had sat in the back beside the wicker picnic basket with its fitted mugs and thermos and played that game of who could see a brown cow first or a pillar box or an AA man on a motor bike. And then there had been that sudden churning in her stomach, and before she could manage to wind down the window she had been sick in the map pocket on the side of the door. She could still see them parked on the verge; all the car doors flung open to let in the air and her father trying to mop up the sick with scrunched balls of newspaper. For weeks afterwards Toby refused to get in the car complaining that it stank.

Every evening her father would come home, pour himself a whisky and sit in the big leather armchair by the fire, while the dog snored next to the grate, and read *The Evening Standard* as he waited for her mother to dish up their dinner, which they would eat alone at the oak table in the dining room; for she and Toby would already have had their high tea in the kitchen and be bound for home-work and bed. After dinner he would retire to his study with his art books and she would be aware of him, through the half-open door at his desk, engrossed in read-ing or writing, surrounded by a purple haze of pipe smoke. She was, she realises, frightened of him. Yet she longed for him to notice her but she is not sure that he even realised she was there half the time. He was more comfortable with his books than with his children.

From an adult perspective, the death of his own father in a building disaster, when he was only twelve, must have had a profound effect. Her grandfather had been a civil engineer on tour in Burma when the bridge he was working on collapsed and four men were killed, buried in a graveyard of steel girders and black mud. It was as if, after that, her father never wanted to get too close to anyone, never trusted that anyone would stay. He and her mother had a strange relationship. They were married for sixty years, though he led a fairly separate life, spending hours at the gallery, and then often staying in town at his club over night. When she was a teenager she even wondered if he might have a mistress. But, she realises, he just needed space apart from the domesticity of his family. Looking back he was, actually, quite dependent on her mother even though she showed little interest in the gallery or art. He would ring several times a day from his office simply to reassure himself that she was still there. And, of course, she always was; in the garden pottering about; or in the kitchen preparing his dinner. That was her role. When she died of pleurisy, suddenly the previous winter, he was lost. After that his descent into confusion was very rapid.

Now she is here she does not know what to do. She is not sure that her presence makes any difference to him. But it does to her, for she has this fantasy that she might still get to know him before it is too late. For old as she is, she still wants his approval and love. She had never felt he liked her very much, was never sure what he wanted from a daughter; but whatever it was, it wasn't her. And he didn't approve of the man she married, had thought him feckless for dropping out of Cambridge and setting up a travelling theatre company, when he could have had a good career at the bar, especially as he had encouraged her to give up her own course. But she'd never really wanted to be a zoologist; zoology was just something she did to fill in the time and, for a while, Clive was so attentive that she had thought he must really love her.

He was glamorous and clever but her father was right, he was feckless; the first of many men in her life in a line of feckless men. At the time she thought it romantic that they'd trekked to the Isle of Wight or Glastonbury to set up their tent for the troupe to perform. Clive had devised a series of alternative versions of Shakespeare's comedies and they crammed the props into their old Morris traveller, which was so rusty you could see the road through a hole in the floor. With its flapping back doors tied with string and wooden lattice framework, like some strange mobile Tudor house sprouting mushrooms and moss, they had been on the road the whole summer. She had worn long Indian skirts and traipsed around in the mud in bare feet, pretending that she didn't mind that Clive was sleeping with the other female performers.

This was the time of free love and she was used to being ignored. But she was a throwback to another century. She believed in romance; in the 'one and only'. She had assumed that this would be Clive, that Clive who would put her, for once in her life, in the limelight. But, of course, that was not what he had in mind. She had felt pulled between the pervading permissiveness of it all and her need for security. Polly was only three months old when he left. She had thought he would see it as his duty to stay, but he had believed it was his right to go. So she had, after all, ended up going back to zoology, to her quiet and uneventful life; had become a teacher in a secondary school to support her daughter. And now, even she was gone, leading her own life. Her father had been furious with Clive, but didn't quite say 'I told you so', though she knew that was what he was thinking. And after that? Well she never chose very well; perhaps hadn't known how to choose men who would stay. After all, she wasn't quite sure what love was supposed to feel like. She was never sure whether it was her fault that she loved too much and too easily or whether it was theirs that they did not love enough.

Outside the weak sun disappears behind a black cloud and the rose beds are suddenly plunged into deep shadow, as the thrush on the wall flies off and, for no apparent reason, her father starts to cry. There is no warning, no apparent external cause, but as he sits staring out of the window he simply begins to sob. She doesn't know what to do. They had never been physically close but she pulls up a chair and sits beside him taking his hand in hers, gently rubbing the clutch of bones in their sheath of dry tight skin. He does not seem to notice and sits rocking slowly backwards and forwards as tears ooze down his papery cheeks. She watches with a mix of terror, revulsion and an overwhelming sense of sadness. She does not know what to do, does not know why he is so upset, as he continues to stare at something in the garden. He becomes more and more agitated, clutching her hand hard now and pulling her towards him. There is a little gurgling sound in his throat as though he is trying to cough up phlegm, or has too much saliva in his mouth, and she can see the stray white hairs poking from beneath the collar of his shirt and growing out of his neck where the nurse who shaved him has missed them. She stands up and, still in his chair, he clings to her like a child, laying his head against her stomach. He has always been a small man, but like many small men he made up for it with his big personality. Now, with its loss, he seems to have shrunk. She freezes. She can feel the convulsions wracking his fragile body and tentatively rests her hands on his thin shoulders. His shoulder blades and ribs protrude from deep beneath the sagging skin and she imagines them jointed and fitted to the now crumbling spine, remembering the small white skeleton of a mouse they had found beneath the rhododendron bush where she and Toby had made a camp; how light and white and pure it seemed.

Without thinking she strokes the thin strands of hair across her father's speckled scalp. They rarely ever embraced, their contact confined to that formal morning kiss. But now he clings to her like Polly used to when she was little and had fallen over or was frightened in the middle of the night by the curtain's flapping shadow or a dream. They stay like this for what seems a long time in the darkening room. She wonders who her father thinks she is, where he has retreated to this man who once used to frighten her and now holds onto her like a baby. Slowly he calms down and loosens his grip, but his face is puffy and there is a strand of spittle caught on his chin. She releases him and goes to the wash basin and picks up the flannel, rinsing it under the tap, then wringing it out and gently wiping his face. Calmer now, he lets her tilt his chin upwards like a compliant child, and bathe it with the warm cloth. His eyes are stained yellow, the whites glutinous as poached eggs. She wonders what is going on behind them, and wishes she could reach out across the best part of fifty years to ask him to do it all again differently.

Then she settles him back in the chair and fetches the ivory brushes and smoothes the dishevelled strands of hair neatly across his scalp, plumps up the cushions behind his back and tries to straighten his jersey and tuck in his shirt that has come out of his trousers aware of his withered flanks. How mortified he would have once been to see himself now. Then it dawns on her that he might be afraid. But that the terror is not so much that of dying, or even the fear of the moment of death but of some impulse, some cry that is forcing itself up from deep inside that understands, yet cannot articulate, how much life has been wasted, how few moments of connection or real tenderness there have been.

And then, for a second, his expression changes. There is something engaged, a flicker of awareness, a recognition as if he does know who she is and wants to beg her forgiveness, to thank her for not giving up on him, for wiping away the dribble and the spit, for being there to acknowledge and witness who he once was, and remind him that he was not always this vacant empty shell. And then he is gone. His face clouds over and he sinks back in his chair staring again out of the window at nothing in particular and her heart lurches. She wants to call out to him to come back and not leave her, to please not leave her, she wants to cling to him, to tell him that she needs him, that she has always needed him. But it is too late.

So this is it. The span and arc of a life. This is what it comes down to, this clutch of years. That is all. A life no different to any other, yet uniquely his; her father's, she thinks, as she sits down beside him and lays her head on his shoulder, breathing in his familiar fragrance, and weeps.

THE HAY WAIN

Janice lifts her head from the table, brought back to the cold kitchen by the small boy's whinging. The stove is out. She gets up straightening herself slowly, taking care with each movement as she clears a space among the used cereal bowls, the stagnant mugs of tea and the blackened frying pan where two bacon rinds lie entombed in their bed of congealed white fat. Her cheek is puffed and her left eye half-closed where the bruise has turned the colour of petrol on water. 'Pack it in, will yer,' she snaps, shoving the brown teat on the bottle of cold tea into the small boy's snot-covered mouth. She shivers. There are no logs. They are stacked in the yard, still green and soaked from the October gales.

'God, what a tip! Darren, fetch me boots.' The toddler obediently waddles off, his soiled nappy dragging round his chubby thighs, and returns from the porch trailing the boots behind him, the bottle still hanging from his mouth like a gun dog's pheasant.

She pulls the black Wellingtons up over her bare mottled legs and splashes her face under the cold tap. The chipped enamel sink is full of potato peelings and tea-leaves and the water stings her inflamed skin. She closes her eyes, letting it wash away the pain, the smell and the hurt and for a moment remembers sitting in Sunday school by the stone font next to the picture of Jesus; a small girl in her best white blouse among the jam jars of Easter forsythia and daffodils. There Our Lord had stood with his gentle face, in his shining halo and long white robe, surrounded by rabbits and deer, baptising sinners and washing away the sins of the world. For the first time in months her eyes fill with tears and she turns her head so her son won't see. She must not let him see.

'Here Darren, give us a hand, there's a good boy,' she says roughly, dabbing her damaged face with the edge of the grubby dishcloth and wiping her nose with the back of her hand. Her body is thin and angular and each movement seems to require an act of will. She goes to the porch and from among the debris of broken deck chairs and muddy boots finds a large cardboard box, which she drags across the kitchen floor to the cupboard under the sink. The stench makes her gag as she opens it onto the pyramid of empty bottles of Newcastle Brown and discarded cans of Tennents Extra.

'Come on Dar, go get yourself a clean nappy, you stink,' she says straightening her back when the box is full, then tying up her lank hair with renewed determination. 'You're too bloody old to poo yourself. Come on pet, come and help me feed the hens.'

Without a word Darren toddles off again, returning with a clean nappy from the pack and lies on his back waving his legs in the air like a dog waiting for its stomach to be rubbed. With his vest pulled up and no nappy, she sees how puny and vulnerable his little body looks. 'I stinks, I stinks,' he croons as she cleans the shit from his small pink buttocks, flushing the contents down the toilet behind the scullery and wrapping the old nappy into a parcel before shoving it into the bin. She secures the new nappy and pulls on a pair of stained dungarees, stuffing the legs into the child's Wellingtons, then spits on the corner of the dish-cloth; with she uses to wipe the encrusted snot off his face. 'Come on then, big boy, you carry the bucket,' she says, going to steady him, laying her rough hand protectively on his tousled head as he picks up the pail of kitchen peelings, staggering proudly under its weight as he spills potato skins and stale bread across the kitchen floor.

'Let's be having that now, it's too heavy for you,' she says, taking the pail and grabbing him by the hand.

The yard is a jumble of rusting car parts and by the fence docks and nettles speckled with black smuts push through the cracked tarmac. A German shepherd dog pulls on its chain snarling at the falling leaves, while on the line between the apple tree and the outhouse the wind snaps at the washing, filling out the drying shirts like the bloated bodies of the drowned.

Janice shoots back the iron bolt of the hens' pen and their boots squelch in the thick mud as the chickens cluster round like nosy spectators at a crash, their red combs wobbling and their scraggy necks bobbing back and forwards.

God, they're stupid, she thinks. 'Chuck 'em some corn, Da,' and a small fist scoops up a handful of grain from the china basin carefully cradled against a woolly blue jumper. Tails up, heads down, the hens scratch at the wet mud. 'Let's get the eggs then, love.'

Calmer now, she is enjoying the ritual of egg collecting with her child and watches as he sticks a grubby hand into the dusty straw of the laying box, feeling for eggs. The hen house smells of bran and shit and the eggs are still warm. She stands back letting him pile them into the empty basin, his small mouth puckered in concentration, as he takes care not to crack them.

Being in the fresh air helps. Being out of that kitchen helps. She knows, now, in her heart of hearts that it is only a matter of time. They go back up to the house. It is not pretty. A cheap post-war bungalow with stucco peeling from the bricks and rusting metal windows frames in need of a lick of paint. By the back door water drips from an overflow pipe leaving a dark green stain down the length of the wall. She has tried to get Mr. Jackson to do something. But there's always an excuse if she goes up to the farm. That's the trouble with tied cottages; no one gives a toss.

She picks up some kindling and a few damp logs. Back in the kitchen she runs the eggs under the cold tap wiping off the lime-white shit, then lays a pile of old rugs on the floor by the stove.

'Time for your nap, Da, come on,' she says pulling off the child's muddy boots and passing him a stained rag comforter, which he winds round his dirty index finger before sticking his thumb in his mouth and curling up under the blankets beside the dog.

She turns back into the kitchen and scrapes the cold bacon out of the white lard and takes a bite. The fat sticks to the roof of her mouth and she tosses it back into the pan. It has been days since she's eaten properly. She makes herself some toast and a mug of Cup-a-soup, then rolls up her sleeves and begins to clear the kitchen. Everything takes a long time because everything hurts. Her face, her lip, her heart. But she has decided. Though how, when she has no money, no place to go? Her chest tightens. Courage. She has to have courage; for her, for Da.

She drags the full box of empties across the yard into the outhouse. She wants them out of sight. She'd believed —had wanted to believe—too many times that it would be different. The outhouse is a litter of rusted lawn mowers and tractor parts. Rope and battery leads lie spewed like innards among the spilt bags of chicken meal and seed potatoes and in the cobwebbed corner behind the broken bicycle is an old tea chest of dusty jam jars.

∼

His face is flushed when he comes in. Not from the previous night's drinking, but from the wind. He has been drilling winter wheat up in the high field by the spinney of hazels. From his tractor cabin on the brow of the hill he can almost see the sea. Up there, alone among the shifting clouds, with a white spinnaker of seagulls billowing behind, he's had time to sober up, to be sorry. Why is it so hard to say the words? He can feel them aching somewhere beneath his ribs. He will try. She isn't a bad girl. His girl, at least. But the minute he sees that purple patchwork spread across her half-closed eye he wants to run, run from her tacit, martyred rebuke. Fuck it; wasn't he out raking muck all day to put a roof over her and the kid's head. Hadn't he married her after she'd got herself knocked up? What did she want? It's more than most of his mates would have done.

He enters the kitchen without a word and pulls off his mud-encrusted boots. He can't look her in the face. She says nothing but he feels the bruise on her cheek like a reproach. He goes and fills the aluminium kettle setting it on the stove, looks around for his tea and sees that there is none but is too proud to say anything, to comment on the newly ordered kitchen, the tidy surfaces, the flowers and berries she has picked in the lane and arranged in a jam jar on the table. He goes instead to the bread bin and hacks himself a thick doorstep of white bread, showering crumbs on the clean surface. Still she says nothing, even when he places the bread directly on the draining board without using a plate, spreading the margarine like a plasterer with the side of the knife and leaving it sticky and unwashed in a pool of jam.

Later that night while lying in bed, she watches the thin wisps of dawn appear over the ridge of the valley. All night she had listened to the wind, like the suck and hiss of the sea high in the copper beeches, as the apples in the orchard drummed against the corrugated roof of the shed. At the height of the gale he had turned to her in his sleep and out of habit rolled over and prized open her legs with his like a pair of scissors, his fingers parting and reaching inside her. She had felt herself unravel. She had wanted to resist, had wanted to remember her anger, but as he'd pushed deeper into the wetness of her, as if reaching for something forgotten, something buried deep within, her legs had flopped open and, against her will, she had melted. It had always been like that. He had only had to touch her for her to forgive him.

That first time she'd seen him she'd been working in The Crown. It had been market day. He'd come to get Mr. Jackson's new carburettor. He'd flirted with her right from the start as she'd pulled pints and he'd stood there by the fruit machine chatting with the other farm lads and some of the boys from the garage, confident and full of brag, thumbs in the belt carriers of his jeans, giving her the eye. That night he'd come back to find her at closing time. Walking with her past the war memorial, down by the Co-op and the path along the back of the playing fields that smelt of dog shit to her parent's bungalow, he had turned and pushed her against the wall, his wet tongue sliding into her mouth, his hand pushing expertly up under her short rucked skirt, so that she'd known, then, that she would never be able to say no to him.

As he climbs on top of her she tries to remember her recent pain and humiliation and goes rigid, her legs closing against him like a lock. He pulls away and turns heavily on his side. She can feel the weight of his rejection, knows that he is hard and aching for her, that he needs something from her that only she can give; not just a fuck, but a cradling, a forgiveness. But he says nothing. Perhaps he really is ashamed; to have beaten her and then tried to enter her, all within twenty-four hours. She stares at the familiar curve of his shoulders, white in the moonlight, the dark curls at the nape of his neck and won't allow herself to think of his touch as she shifts further across to her side of the bed.

∿

She sees it by chance advertised on a card in the post office while she is collecting the family allowance. *Caravan to Let*. That morning there's a frost as she lies in bed pretending to sleep when he rises at five for the milking, shuffling round the dark room, pulling on his stiff jeans, his mud-spattered shirt and sweater from where he's dropped them the night before on the floor. He doesn't speak, but she can feel his silent anger hard as anthracite. She waits till he's left. The house is freezing. There are still no dry logs. She boils a kettle and washes beneath her breasts and armpits, dabbing round the purple bruise. Then she wakes Darren, washes him and makes him a fresh bottle of milky tea, puts on his outdoor clothes and straps him into his buggy.

The track from the cottage is pockmarked with holes. The wheels of the buggy spin in the puddles, catching on the protruding stones. The ground is warming and a thin white mist rises like steam across the fields. The cows, turned out after milking, lollop towards the gate, their kohl-rimmed eyes glassy with curiosity, their pink noses running like snotty children's.

It's a three-mile walk to Great Ash. No buses go across country, only one early in the morning into town, and an extra one on market day. Most people in the village have cars, big estates with room for their kids and the dog. But they aren't local people. She used to enjoy market days. She'd meet Sharon and Tanya by the war memorial. They'd often gone there for a quick fag when they'd bunked off maths from school. Now if they have enough money they go to the chip shop or sit and watch the kids play in the sand pit in the playground while they chat about their blokes or look through the catalogue, marking what they'd buy if they had enough money; an electric foot spa, a heated hostess trolley, they giggle.

Sometimes she takes Darren to the cattle market to watch the young steers being auctioned. He likes the yard where they sell rabbits in cages, where, in fact, they sell anything; broken electric fires, twin tubs, garden shears, mildewed books and pictures with broken frames from house clearances. It had been there that she'd once seen an old biscuit tin she'd liked. It had a picture on the lid of an old fashioned hay wagon pulled by a team of horses crossing a shallow stream. There was a man standing on the back and opposite a house that looked like a mill. A small dog, a black and white spaniel, was barking on the bank and in the distance on the right she could see a group of farm workers making hay. She'd stopped to pick it up, wondering where it was. The place didn't look local. It must have been painted a long time ago. The country looked nothing like that now. There was a big scratch down one side where someone must have put something heavy on it. It ran all the way through the stormy sky down into the flat hay field. One day she would live in a house where everything was brand new.

~

It's at the bottom of an orchard. There's a rickety bed, a cooker of sorts, a Formica topped table and paraffin stove. Ninety-five quid deposit, then forty-five a week, and that's only because winter's coming and he's a soft touch. He'd get double in the summer. Her heart sinks. She tells him she doesn't have the money.

'Up to you, love. That's the price. You can always get in touch if you change your mind. Young girl like you, should be ways and means,' he says locking the door behind him with his big meaty hand, a gold sovereign flashing on of his middle finger. 'See what you can do,' he winks, jangling the large bunch of keys in his trouser pocket.

It's taken her an hour and a half to get there with Darren crying and squirming in the buggy. She watches the man climb back into his Ford Sierra and wonders if she should call out and stop him. But she cannot. It would be more than she could bear, she thinks, watching as he pulls out of the gate, the small toy dog nodding frantically at her from the back window. She walks back down the lane. The mist has turned to drizzle. She doesn't have an umbrella and her thin jacket is soaked through. But it's her only chance. Her parents won't have her back. After she'd fallen for Daren in her last term at school they'd chucked her out. You've made your bed, girl. Now you lie in it. How could she get ninety-five bloody quid?

It's dinnertime when they finally trudge back up the track. She manages to find a few dry logs to light the stove to fry Darren and herself each an egg, dipping in the remains of the stale toasted loaf. Outside the dog is barking, pulling on his chain demanding to be fed. She goes to him, fills his bowl and waters the hens. The yard is littered with windfalls from last night's gales; their smashed innards a mush on the muddy concrete. She begins to chuck them over the wall into the field when suddenly she remembers the jam jars in the barn.

∼

He can't understand her new self-assurance. Make neither head nor tail of it. There is something different about her. She hardly speaks, just drifts around the house like a bloody ghost. She won't cook for him and moves out of their room in with Darren, sleeping beside him under his Thomas the Tank engine duvet in his narrow baby-bed. In the past he'd have threatened, got heavy, asked her who the fuck she thought she was, playing silly buggers. But now, something inside of him is afraid of something new in her. He can't stand her silence. He feels safe with their rows, knows how to ride them, how to soften her with a touch. Now he hardly comes home, feels like an intruder in his own house, even with the little lad when he reaches to pat him on the head with his oily hand and he senses him pull away. After work he goes straight to the pub, sitting morosely over a pint watching the match. It's as though there's an invisible electric fence between them. Christ, what if his friends find out. He'll be a laughing stock. All right for some, then, Kev, this getting married malarkey, getting your leg over whenever you fancy, they'd joked at The Crown, downing pints and staggering out of the pub into the pavement on his stag night.

She works when Darren is asleep, rinsing and scalding the jars with boiling water, turning them upside down on clean tea towels spread on the scrubbed deal table. There are so many apples she wonders if she can gather them all before they rot. Peeling them is slow work. She tries quartering them or taking the skin off in a spiral, allowing herself a wish if she manages not to break it. She hardly knows what she's wishing for; for it all to be mended, for him to love her again and to stop drinking, to be free. She bleaches the inside of the big aluminium pan which she uses for boiling the hens' scraps, and then swills it out with hot water. It's the only pan she has that's big enough. She adds chopped onion, raisins, vinegar, spices; all bought on her last trip to town, which she'd hidden in the cupboard under the stairs. She hadn't dare buy the stuff at the post office stores in the village. She remembers exactly how her Nan had done it, remembers standing on the kitchen stool by the range when she had been small helping her stir the brown liquid with a wooden spoon.

A sweet acrid smell fills the kitchen; exotic spices, cinnamon, nutmeg and mace. Smells of places she'll never visit. When Darren wakes she lets him help her pour the dark liquid into the jars. Then she covers the neck of each with a disc of wax paper and seals them with plastic film and a rubber band. On each new white label she writes: *Apple Chutney. October.*

For the next week she chops fruit and fills jars whenever she has the chance, flinging open the windows to get rid of the cloying smell. She needn't have worried. He avoids her as much as possible. She hides the jars deep in the back of Darren's cupboard, behind the Lego and his old carry cot. She feels both strong and afraid. She's not used to secrets. Even when she fell pregnant with Da she'd told Sharon. But now she is the only person in the world who knows of her plan. She tries to imagine her life without him and her heart stumbles. She'd wanted him so much, knew that Sharon had been green when she'd told her and Tanya about the night behind the playing field.

'Go on Jan, tell us. Did you do it? Did you? Bet he's fucking great. God, Kevin Thomson; you're a right lucky cow.'

Clearing a space on the furthest shelf, she finds them wrapped in yellowing tissue. The white satin sling-backs she'd worn on her wedding day. She sits down among the jumble of baby clothes and toys and unwraps them, turning them over and over, examining the thin heels, the gently curved instep and polished satin. Quickly she wraps them up again tossing them deep in the back of the cupboard, as if they might hook her back in, melt her resolve. If she softens now, she knows she will be done for. That's how it's always been. Her hand reaches for her face, the ragged scar across her brow; her badge of courage. Since that night when he'd caught her by the hair and beaten her face against the edge of the table after she'd asked him, yet again, for meter money to heat the freezing house, knowing that he'd spent what he should have given her in the pub, she'd seen no one. How could she have explained? She'd have been too ashamed. They would say she must have done something to deserve it; a nice looking fella like that. Any of the girls would have had him. On TV she'd seen that in towns there were places for women like her to go.

But here? In the middle of nowhere?

She fills the wheelbarrow with as many jars as it will take and still she has a load more. She can't believe she's cut and scrubbed so many apples. On top of these she balances a wide plank, four bricks and a checked table-cloth and sets up her stall at the top of the track lining up the jars neatly beside a basket of freshly laid eggs. On a piece of card she writes: *Homemade chutney. Free range eggs*, with one of Darren's felt-tips, while he sits strapped in his buggy sucking at his bottle of cold tea. God, she hopes none of the other farm workers come past and tell Kev. She knows it's a risk.

Half an hour passes and a few cars sail by, and the odd tractor dropping dollops of slurry in the frozen puddles. Her flimsy jacket is useless against the raw chill as she walks up and down stamping her feet to keep warm. Then a silver Volvo pulls up and a young woman in a green wax jacket and loosely knotted woollen scarf gets out. Her blond hair is cut in a bob like a single piece of polished silk.

'How lovely. Homemade? Did you make it yourself?' she asks, picking up the amber jars. Her voice is soft and Janice notices her sweet scent like orange blossom and vanilla.

'How clever,' the young woman continues, hardly drawing breath. 'I'd never have the time. They're perfect. My friends in London will love them. Something special from the country. And the eggs, are they from your own hens?'

Janice nods and smiles, placing the jars in the woman's wicker basket, alongside two boxes of eggs, which she shuts in the back next to two yapping King Charles spaniels.

'How much is that? What a bit of luck I spotted you. I nearly drove past. You're very easy to miss.'

Then the door slams and the wheels of the Volvo spin and skid in the mud as the young woman turns and drives off towards the main road. Janice opens her icy fingers onto a ten-pound note, a pound coin and a fifty pence piece, slipping the money into her pocket and wrapping her thin coat tightly around her narrow frame. She is freezing and Darren has started to cry. She tries to quieten him, slowly rocking the buggy backward and forwards as more cars speed past, their wheels throwing up fans of muddy spray. They have a long day ahead.

THE LAUGHING
CAVALIER

Well here I am. 55 years, 29 days and roughly one hour old. It's a Monday afternoon. Monday the 3rd April at 3.30 to be precise and it's raining. As I look out of my study window into the garden, the foliage that burst into over-optimistic leaf in the untimely heat wave is dripping and sodden, like the clothes of a party goer who's got drunk and fallen into the host's swimming pool and now simply looks embarrassed and bedraggled. The pink almond blossom on the tree at the far end of the garden is being blown off its branches like wet confetti, the sort that sticks to pavements outside municipal register offices, and then lies bleeding away its colour, bleached and muddy among the tacky little silver paper horse shoes.

I'm lucky, I suppose, that I look young for my age. Well certainly now that I've lost half a stone on the Atkins diet,

I do. Cut out the carbs and simply eat protein and it will fall off, the book said. Well it did at first. Then it just stopped. You also have to take linseed for your bowels so that you end up feeling like a budgerigar chomping through a plateful with your fried eggs and bacon each morning, and it sticks between the teeth. The little husks wedge themselves there so that even flossing and brushing fails to remove them. Anyway, too much protein leads to constipation and who wants to be thin and then die of bowel cancer?

I keep trying to convince myself that if I lose another half stone and get really fit—all those sit ups I keep doing in the drab council gym that smells of stale trainers, along with the pilates curls on my bedroom floor first thing in the morning—that my life will change, that I will meet someone and fall in love. Some might say it's rather late in the day. Some—more charitably—might say better late than never. But the truth is, it is not enough to fall in love. No, that's what I have always done, and it's like becoming ill, getting flu. It creeps up on you when you least expect it and knocks you sideways so that you can barely function. Then there are all those weeks of convalescence and feeling below par when it all goes wrong or is not reciprocated, of waiting by the phone like a hapless girl for him to ring and then, when he doesn't or fobs you off with excuses about work or seeing his children, phoning the few friends who are loyal enough to listen to you being obsessive and boring. After all, there is nothing so apparently sad, so open to ridicule as a lovelorn middle-aged woman. The delirium of love is fine in the young, but in the middle-aged? It's just ridiculous.

The trouble is that I don't feel middle-aged, not on the inside anyway, and on good days I don't even look it. Well not after 11.00 am, if I have been to bed early, not had half a bottle of wine the night before and drunk plenty of water to prevent bags under my eyes, I don't. No, falling in love is not enough. I have to meet someone who also wants to fall in love with me. Yes, you've got it. I want the grand passion before I claim my bus pass.

It's nonsense, of course. That's the sort of thing you can believe when you are 25, but at 55? What are you supposed to believe at 55? Isn't it supposed to be a time of consolidation? Shouldn't one more properly be offering one's time to the committee of the local branch of NSPCC or joining the National Trust? Others are planning to retire and find a remote ruin in Andalucía or Umbria to do up with their husbands who also, now, have plenty of time on their hands, to turn into a family holiday home so that the grandchildren can come and stay in the summer. Though strictly speaking, as a writer I have nothing to retire from and I don't have a husband or grandchildren, let alone enough money to buy a holiday home.

Appropriate things to do once you are over 50:

- go on a Saga holiday
- get cheaper car insurance, but I don't have a car so that's not an option
- plan where you will go on days out when you finally get your freedom pass

- start cultivating a vegetable patch
- go on a cruise
- throw out your thongs

And what do I want to do? Really want to do? Do I really want to fall in love again? As I say, I've done it countless times but always with the wrong men, men who have held back, men who wouldn't commit, men who—in truth—didn't really love me though for a while seemed happy enough to inhabit the other side of my bed. And well, I was married once. But that's another story.

No, what I want is a last grand *folie à deux*; the meeting of hearts and minds and bodies. Otherwise what is the point of all this exercise and healthy eating, of checking the glycaemic index of everything I consume, of forgoing that other glass of Rioja? I might as well just go down like the proverbial Titanic, stately and massive, under an indulgence of Black Forest cheese cake or Death by Chocolate gateau. All this restraint has to be for something. But I don't just want to settle for someone with whom to push the trolley round Tesco and argue with about who has most of the duvet or even whose turn it is to take the dog for a walk—that's if I had a dog, which I don't. Actually, I don't particularly like them very much, dogs, I mean—too demanding, too dependent, too smelly. I'd really rather have a man.

But what worries me about this business of getting older is, well it's obvious, isn't it? Apart from the slackening skin, it's the lack of time. It's like being an Olympic runner on the last lap, there may still be a way to go before the end of the race but suddenly you can see the finishing line off up in the distance and you realise that most of the track is now behind you. One day you wake up and realise that the thing you have spent your whole life getting used to — being young — is over, used up. It's a shock. Somehow you think in your heart that you will be exempt. That aging is what happens to other people; people who are careless or ought to know better. But suddenly there you are having to face the prospect that the thing you most want may never happen; that you might die and never experience it. After all, people die suddenly, just like that, all the time; from falling off a ladder, in a car crash or from swallowing a fish bone; presumably many of them with ambitions and wish-lists still unfulfilled: a longing to climb in the Himalayas or learn the flute.

And why am I sitting here looking into the wet garden? Well, that's what I am supposed to do. Sit and write. That is the decision that I've made. My Faustian pact. This is my life. But nothing is ever that simple.

Maybe I could, if I chose, imagine it differently. Growing old with my husband, someone I've been with for 30 years, someone whose collar size I remember, someone who I know hates liver and would prefer to read biographies rather than fiction and drink red wine rather than white. Someone who will only wear pure wool socks and refuses to buy bottled mineral water because he says it's a waste of money and bad for the environment and that if it's left to stand in the bottle for a day it develops more bugs than the water in the tap. Someone who is still rude about my driving and who many years ago had an affair with his secretary, but whom I forgave and who has been grateful ever since that the daily tenor of our lives, our weekends with our grandchildren, the Sunday morning sherry *concerts* we occasionally go to at the Wigmore Hall, and the companionable silence sitting on the sofa with a glass of whisky before bed watching *Newsnight* means he doesn't have to face growing old alone or shop in Tesco's for frozen meals for one.

Well that's one version of how it might have been at least.

I try to imagine being really old. Sound in mind, perhaps, but not in body, living in a care home, say, in Bexhill-on-Sea, my children all in far flung places getting on with their lives as children must, passing my days reading books from the library trolley, avoiding the quizzes and the bingo with the other residents in the day room that smells of orchid air freshener, which barely covers the incipient odour of urine. Residents who think I'm stuck up because I like to read real literature and don't watch daytime TV, who are presided over by a cheap print of Franz Hals' *Laughing Cavalier* in a nasty plastic frame that looks down over the incontinent and dazed with an expression that some would describe as jovial but others might, in the circumstances, consider one of cynical mockery. It hangs over the piano that's played once a week by the music therapist to encourage the confused to remember the songs of their youth. *All you need is love da de da de da . . .*

Or I imagine sitting at the window looking out across the flat expanse of concrete, where the nurses park their cars and hide behind the bins to have a quick fag, which leads down to the promenade and the corrugated grey waves of the English Channel. I remember going there once, to Bexhill that is. I can't remember why. The first shop I passed when I got off the train was a chiropodist's. In the window there was a sign offering toe nail clipping for half-price to senior citizens on Wednesday afternoon's after 3.00pm. Perhaps for some that was the highlight of their week. The next shop but one was a funeral parlour. No wonder they called it *Costa Geriatrica*. All along the promenade there were old people sitting in deckchairs or wheel chairs with rugs over their bent knees, old men with arthritic hands in polyester drip-dry trousers and old ladies with tight blue perms through which you could see the thin white skin of their skulls, watching the beach flag snap in the wind and the seagulls scavenging the crumbs of their carelessly dropped scones.

The thing about places like that is that they must be full of people who once had dreams. They may all look as though they are waiting to die but some of them must have once had grand passions or secrets in their lives; the clandestine adultery, the illegitimate child or an incestuous love. I can imagine sitting in the corner of the conservatory with my book, a frail, unremarkable old lady, as the nurses and carers go about the business of handing out mid-morning tea and Rich Tea biscuits. Young women from the Philippines or Jamaica working anti-social hours for insufficient money, who long for the sun and the taste of sweet potatoes cooked the way their grandmothers once did, young women who could imagine nothing of my life, or the hunger I'd once had in my 50s for the young Kosovan student I'd met at the Royal Festival Hall when I had gone one Easter to hear Bach's Saint Mathew Passion.

Why had I been there? Because I was lonely and because music connects us to emotions that it's not possible to express in any other way than through sex or love. I'd been sitting in the cheap seats reading the programme notes when he'd come in late, much to the tuts and annoyance of the rest of the row, who having settled down now had to stand up again clutching jackets and bags. When he sat down in the seat beside me I hardly noticed him. But then, as the concert went on, I'd become aware of his hands resting on the knees of his jeans, the long fingers, the vulnerable bony joints, the knuckles straining against the slightly tanned skin. Once I'd noticed them I couldn't take my eyes off them. I could simply have reached out and taken his hand and slipped my fingers between his. By the end of the concert I knew those hands as well as I would know other bits of his body during the next three months. I could hear his breathing below the swell of the choir, smell the acid tang of his skin, and see the muscles tighten in his cheek when suddenly the singers broke into the two antiphonal choruses and the voices of the choir sang out with, 'O Lamb of God Most Holy', piercing through all the private pain hidden within that hall with the promise of redemption, so that my heart lurch like something woken out of a long sleep

How would anyone entering that day room of the care home on that particular morning and seeing a grey haired old woman reading know that she had once lain naked in the dim light of evening with a beautiful long limbed boy in his bed-sit in Dalston, while he lay with his head on her stomach speaking of his dreams. He had wanted to go to film school, to return to Kosovo to make a documentary about what he'd witnessed during the war, go back to the villages where there had been ethnic cleansing to try to understand why neighbour had turned on neighbour, friend on friend. He had already spent a year studying in London but now had run out of money and worked as a waiter in a bar in Hoxton. One day it would be different; I'd be able to say I'd known him before he was famous. One day he'd go back and do something worthwhile, he said, before running his tongue along my inner thigh.

And why me? Why had he chosen me, an older woman, a woman past her prime, whose stomach, despite the sits ups, would always show the stretch marks and flab of childbearing? Because I just happened to be there that's all. Who said that, Bob Dylan? Because when my Kosovan was listening to Bach in the seat next to mine there was a tacit connection of pain and mutual longing; because he wanted the comfort of my body so much, because unlike the young girls he'd known I listened to him and he was so very grateful.

Fantasies. It's easy to get side-tracked. That's what writers do, create fantasies. Sometimes they feel more real than the lives we lead. But we are not, it seems, the only ones. In a bid to further the cause of falling in love, I logged onto a dating website. Yes, I admit it. After all, where am I supposed to find him, this object of my desires? In the checkout in Sainsbury's, in the rush hour crush on the Piccadilly line? And yesterday I went and met the man who had been emailing me for while. He had a lot of degrees. Degrees in social anthropology, in archaeology and I forget what else. M Phils. and D Litts. So he must have been clever and I like clever men, but it was still a mistake. His photograph had only shown his face. But like an iceberg, two thirds of him remained hidden beneath the level of the camera lens. Two thirds or, in his case, at least 18 stone. I was sitting in Patisserie Valerie in Soho toying with a black coffee when he arrived puffing and sweating and dabbing his reddened face with a handkerchief. He had just cycled, he said. Several miles. He was wearing track suit bottoms. Track suit bottoms that were too short and too tight. Who wears track suit bottoms on a date, especially if you are 18 stone? But I had said I would meet him and it felt like a duty to be as pleasant as I could possibly be. So I smiled and kept smiling and talking as the conversation lapsed and he poured yet another packet of sugar into his cappuccino, stirring it round vigorously in the chocolaty foam. I couldn't take my eyes of his hands. Perhaps I have a thing about men's hands. Sometimes I still remember those of my Kosovan, caressing and insistent, but his were spongy, dimpled and white, rather small without any knuckles and nails that were just a little too long; hands like an old woman's. I had to be nice to him because I felt so sorry for him. His hands said everything. A clever man who had never had any life, a clever man who had let himself become 18 stone, who had never been married, who had no children and was impressed by me. Me, a woman of 55 who wishes she was still 40 with a future. A woman who ,as she sits and talks to him, wishes desperately she was somewhere else.

Perhaps I should just give in gracefully. That's what lots of women I know have done. They've abandoned that part of their life and with it shut the door on push up-bras and lacy black thongs for comfortable M&S big knickers. The Bus Pass Bridget Jones. They are happy walking with the Ramblers on Sundays and are not bothered about exposing themselves to the sun and getting lines or buying ridiculously expensive moisturisers which can't possibly do what they promise. Yet so many of them, whose husbands have left for other younger, blonder more nubile models, seem like the brigade of the abandoned.

If there is something sad about the lovelorn middle-aged woman, then there's something even sadder about giving up hope. For what is love or sex but the life force? The green fuse. Writing, sex, love. The holy trinity.

And now? Well I'm back looking out of the window above my rain soaked garden. Opposite there's a brick wall and a bush of forsythia smothered in tiny yellow stars and the garden chair I should have put away for the winter, which has now become water-logged. Next door the black and white cat is sheltering under the bike shed. It's a pity that the daffodils I planted are being smashed by the relentless rain. All that effort to grow and just as they reach their moment of glory, wham, they're struck down. I used to enjoy gardening once, but that was in another life long ago, a country life with small brown children chasing each other naked across speedwell covered lawn and making rainbows with the garden spray in the summer sunlight by a line of newly hung washing.

That was the life of a young woman who still believed in a future; a future which lay ahead mostly unwritten. How did so much time pass?

I have to stop this daydreaming and get back to work. I have a deadline. Writing; that's what I do now. I make things up. I tell stories. Perhaps, after all, it shouldn't be Bexhill but Brighton, and maybe I should choose another painting rather than the *Laughing Cavalier*—Picasso's *Crying Woman* for example. But I think I will keep my Kosovan. I've grown rather fond of him. Perhaps if I go on writing I will find out a bit more about him.

Outside it has stopped raining now and a fat blackbird, bathing in a puddle, is shaking off the droplets from its wet feathers, before spreading its wings and flying off over the fence into the neighbour's garden.